MISSION:

~impossible to~

SURRENDER

THE IMPOSSIBLE MISSION SERIES · Book Two

JACKI DELECKI

MORE BOOKS BY JACKI DELECKI

THE IMPOSSIBLE MISSION SERIES
Contemporary Romantic Suspense
Mission: Impossible to Resist
Mission: Impossible to Surrender
Mission: Impossible to Love
(coming June 2019)

THE GRAYCE WALTERS SERIES
Contemporary Romantic Suspense
An Inner Fire
Women Under Fire
Men Under Fire
Marriage Under Fire
A Marine's Christmas Wedding
The Grayce Walters Series Set

THE CODE BREAKERS SERIES
Regency Period Romantic Suspense
A Code of Love
A Christmas Code
A Code of the Heart
A Cantata of Love
A Wedding Code
A Code of Honor
A Holiday Code for Love
The Code Breakers Set

Find all of Jacki's books on her website.
https://jackidelecki.com/books/

ACKNOWLEDGMENTS

Thank you to my "team" of experts who shared their incredible knowledge, enthusiasm, and unique abilities with me. I'm most grateful for their gifts of time and expertise. Any errors are my own mistakes or my imagination run amok: Sergey Smirnov, Beth Irwin, and Captain (P) Cory Kastl, United States Army.

And to my "team" who offer their incredible skills and support: Mary-Theresa Hussey, editor extraordinaire, Karuna, my brilliant plot partner, Maria Connor and Erica Monroe, who keep me organized—not an easy task. Thank you.

To my husband—my hero!

CHAPTER ONE

Sophie bolted upright in bed, terror gripping her chest. Had she screamed aloud? Her rapid, panicky breathing was the only sound in the cold, silent night. Disoriented, she shivered, peering into the blackness. The sweet fragrance of Titepatti and Sunpatti leaves prickled her nose.

She inhaled the scent of the tender Himalayan leaves burning in an incense vessel to keep the evil spirits away. She focused on slowing her racing heart, telling herself she was here, safe and sound in Nepal, away from the memories.

The sense of peacefulness settling her trembling body was shattered by another agonizing scream. Every nerve ending jolted into action. Sophie jumped from the wooden pallet. Ignoring the burning candle, she clicked the flashlight on her phone, and rushed along the long wooden passage, the keening cry pulsing through her. It had to be Tariq, the young refugee boy from Pakistan who had recently been moved to the monastery.

Sophie followed the sound to the door in the guest side of the temple, slowly opening the door. She knelt next to the boy's cot and ran her hand over his mussed ebony hair. "Tariq, it's me. Sophie."

Although still asleep, the rough sheet was twisted in his hands. The same sweet incense burned next to his bed. Speaking in the boy's Punjabi dialect, Sophie crooned, "You're safe."

The ten-year-old opened his eyes and stared at Sophie. By his jagged breathing and the confusion in his dark eyes as he searched her face—he was still trapped in his nightmare.

"You're in Nepal with Bhikshu Bunan." Sophie stopped herself from saying, "Not in Lahore" fearing to stir up painful memories. His parents and sister had died in an Ahmadiyya mosque bombing. He had been living with relatives until recently when he was able to flee to Nepal's refugee camps.

"The fire…"

There had been an unexplained fire near where Tariq had lived in the camp. Sophie didn't know all the details, only that Bunan had brought the boy to stay at the monastery.

She patted his arm. "It was a bad dream. I have them too." Like Tariq, she had demons. Being the daughter of one of the world's richest men didn't guarantee safety.

"Sophie?" The boy's dark eyes tracked her face. "Is it time to leave?"

Was Tariq ill? Or confused because of his latest trauma due to the fire? He wasn't leaving. Sophie lit the candle on the boy's nightstand. Sophie was leaving tomorrow after trekking throughout Nepal for two months and volunteering in several refugee camps.

"You don't believe me?" Tariq giggled, bringing a moment of joy into the endless, cold night.

The resilient youth was already bridging the dread of nightmares to the welcoming light of tomorrow's promises. Sophie always thought of herself as resilient, but now, after the kidnapping, she was no longer sure.

"I'm going with you to Seattle."

Poor Tariq, she sighed with remorse. She wished she could take the spirited boy with her, but his future, uncertain as it might be, was here. To cope with her departure, he was spinning a fantasy. Sophie had done the same thing when her mother had died. She'd made up stories about where her mother had gone and when she'd return, and how Sophie would regale her with tales of adventures.

"Tariq, you live here in Kathmandu with Bhikshu Bunan. I'll come back to visit."

Since she was the only one to master his Lahore regional dialect, she had become close to the irrepressible youth. She always had a facility for language and since spending time in the camps with refugees from Bhutan, Somalia, and Pakistan, she had mastered the subtleties of the various refugee dialects. Or maybe removed from the frantic pace of daily life, she had truly listened.

"Bunan wants me to go with you to an island where I'll live with a wise friend of Uncle Parvez. Bunan said you will take me to this island because you're a good woman. And you will protect me until I get there."

Sophie now felt as if she were the one in a dream state. She almost pinched herself. Was she awake? Nepal had that effect on you, the looming ominous mountains, the deep silent awareness, and profound religious faith, had you believing in another dimension, another realm.

"But he hasn't said anything to me."

"He wants to surprise you." And there was the incorrigible giggle again.

Sophie was trying to piece together what the monk had told her about Tariq's family. Now she realized she knew close to nothing except Tariq had traveled with a distant relative, making his way to Nepal to escape religious persecution. The Ahmadiyya Muslims were considered heretics because they believed in another prophet who came after Mohammed. "Why aren't you safe here?" She didn't understand all the politics among the various refugees in Nepal.

"I should go back to sleep. We leave early tomorrow. Bhikshu Bunan told me that Uncle Harry will come in your father's very fast jet. And I will like Uncle Harry a lot. He will be like my Uncle Parvez who took me from Pakistan."

Tariq referred to the distant relative who had brought him into Bhikshu Bunan's sphere as uncle as a sign of respect as she did with Uncle Harry, the head of her family's security.

"Now Uncle Harry will take me to America."

Even wide awake, Sophie was confounded. Bhikshu Bunan would never make promises without consulting her. The monk had told Tariq about her Uncle Harry who had always been there for Sophie after her mother died and during her acting-out phase. Recalling the sight of Uncle Harry, sprawled on the ground in front of her, unconscious with blood pouring out of the gaping hole in his chest, dark dread shuddered down her spine. He had stepped in front of the shooter in an effort to stop her kidnapping.

During the time she was held by the kidnappers, she suffered the profound guilt in believing that Uncle Harry had died protecting her. And had rejoiced to find him alive.

Tariq's black eyes shuttered closed as he squeezed Sophie's hand. "You love Uncle Harry like I loved my uncle. Tomorrow I go to America."

A bewildered Sophie watched the boy fall back to sleep with his lips turned up in a small smile.

How could she crush his dreams? She couldn't take him with her. She wasn't his legal guardian. She didn't even know who that might be. Tariq didn't have an American passport or a visa or any legal way to enter the country. Her heart thrashed against her chest like a caged bird at the thought of his disappointment in the morning. Her own childhood had been filled with disappointment and she'd never want Tariq to have his heart broken.

She needed to speak with Bhikshu Bunan. Was this some sort of test? This was going too far by the monk. She wouldn't allow Bunan to smile calmly at her and ask her to trust. The tender heart of a young boy was at stake. Not a lesson for a mistrustful, weary woman.

She softly kissed the boy's cheek and left to confront the monk. She had to figure this out before Tariq awoke again.

CHAPTER TWO

Finn Jenkins stepped out of the sleek, supersonic Gulf Stream jet and concentrated on masking the pain of his abdominal wound with each step down to the tarmac. Traveling fourteen thousand miles round-trip between Seattle and Nepal while still in recovery might be a bit extreme, but SEALs were trained to do extreme. The chance to be with Sophie over the next eight hours return to Seattle was worth the trip.

Finn scoured the area, hyper-vigilant for anyone or anything out of place in the private section of Kathmandu's Tribhuvan International Airport. The visceral memory of Sophie's capture just months ago by the infamous Chinese 14K Triad was worse than any stab wound. And all because he had left her to check on the hired security in Hong Kong.

Never going to happen again, not on his watch. Not that Sophie would like hearing that her arrivals and departures were planned as if she were an exceedingly valuable package—compliments of her father's billions—and also a much loved package.

Finn heard the alert ping of a new text and saw that Reeves, the family's security IT genius, had sent a message. What did Reeves mean that Sophie had a surprise that Finn wasn't going to like? Was her surprise that she was with Alex Hardy, the damn famous rock star? He had heard that Hardy had followed her to Nepal. Finn's plan to get Sophie used to him in her life while he worked some things out might have just blown up like a M67 grenade, shattering his dreams into unrecognizable fragments.

Finn ground his teeth, a habit he thought he had left behind. He was going to kick Reeves's ass for taunting him. Panic, an unknown and unacknowledged feeling for a highly trained operator, twisted in his gut.

A black SUV pulled up at the gate. Finn checked his watch— right on time. Nick, his older brother, climbed out of the SUV, scanning the entire area, reinforcing that everyone was vigilant about Sophie's safety.

Nick had taken over coordinating Sophie's months in Nepal while Finn was on a mission. It had been a joint military training mission to assist the *Batallones de Comandos*, Mexico's counterpart to SEALS, who were rounding up a deadly drug cartel in the Baja California Sur. Training mission, his ass. More like a setup. Finn had finished off the cartel shooter who had killed the *Mexican Commando*, but not before the guy had sliced and diced Finn's abdomen.

A familiar warmth spread through him watching Sophie climb out of the SUV, baring her shapely legs. She smiled and waved when she saw Finn. He nodded, trying to act like he had his shit together. He moved toward Sophie, wanting to sweep her into his arms and swing her in a circle but his stitched-up abdomen wouldn't allow it. He kept his steps even and unrushed as he tried to hide his feelings. He was an expert in hiding his love for Sophie.

"Finn, I've a surprise for you," Sophie chirped from ten feet away, her light voice taking on the familiar teasing lilt, triggering his need for this woman, and only this woman. Over the years he'd thought his feelings would fade. She was too young, their lives too different. And then he'd seen her last year and had been rocked to his core.

He had barely resisted blurting out his feelings when she'd been shaken and vulnerable from the abduction. Fear blocked out the pleasure of seeing Sophie, with her blonde curls swinging around her shoulders, her violet baby blues, and her childhood habit of worrying her lower lip between her teeth when she was nervous or excited.

Finn was closing the space between them when another black SUV roared through the open gate onto the private tarmac. Finn dove to cover Sophie while pulling out the SIG 229 compact pistol tucked into the back of his jeans. He rolled her against the side of the SUV, her body trembling as he wedged her between him and the SUV, placing himself in front with his gun drawn as she lay on the ground.

"Finn?" Sophie's voice came out in a timid whisper, a voice he recognized when she'd looked to him for reassurance as a young girl. He reached back and squeezed her hand.

He listened for the tat-tat of assault rifles, to estimate the count of shooters. His brother and Sophie's detail were experienced operators and could take out one SUV and its occupants. He wouldn't leave Sophie unprotected. Not this time. With no gunfire erupting, nothing but doors slamming and the sound of Nick, the calm brother, shouting, Finn removed his finger off the trigger on his SIG. If Nick was pissed off, there was no threat. Because if there was danger, Nick would be eerily calm, in a deadly zone.

"What the hell, Hardy?" Nick's voice pitched higher. Just 210 pounds of an ex-Marine pissed off by the arrival of the rock star.

"God, man. I'm sorry. I just wanted to see Sophie before she took off. How would I know you'd go all terminator on me?"

Finn took a calming breath and another to try to counter the adrenaline rush. However, the urge to tear Hardy apart, if there was anything left of the musician once Nick finished, wasn't helping. Lowering his weapon, Finn twisted to help Sophie get up. "Sorry, Soph, for the crazy."

Her hands were over her face. Was she going to cry? Finn regretted throwing Sophie down and upsetting her, but he knew he'd do it again in the same situation.

He was going to kick someone's ass for not closing the gate after Sophie's arrival. It was jolting Sophie back to the moment when she had been taken.

"I'm really sorry, Soph." Finn wanted to touch her but waited, watching as she began to shake.

"Soph?"

Sophie removed her hands, barely able to get the words out before she started laughing. "You couldn't just say duck or something?"

Eight hours of travel was worth this exact moment—Sophie's grin, her bright eyes wide in total amusement—lightening his world-weary heart.

Finn grinned back before brushing a curl behind her ear. "Not exactly the way I planned to say hello."

"And I thought I was going to be the one with the surprise." Sophie jerked away. "Oh, my God. I hope he's not frightened."

Finn scrambled to his feet, ignoring the yank on his sutures. "You better go save your boyfriend before Nick kills him." He gave her a hand up, the warmth of her small hand wrapped in his made him want to hold on and never let go.

"Sophie, are you all right?" Hardy rushed toward them. The singer's man bun, open denim shirt, and tight-fitting jeans were classic Sophie. Finn was glad that he had been out of the country and hadn't witnessed teenaged Sophie in her wild musician phase. The stress of the kidnapping had pushed her back down a familiar path.

Finn caught Nick's amused grin usually, unflappable SEAL operator's overreaction. Finn couldn't tell anyone that he wasn't totally recovered from the fear when he'd thought he'd lost Sophie. Shrugging his shoulders, Finn sauntered toward Nick, not making any attempt to hide his shit-eating grin. Yeah, all his brothers were going to hear about this escapade.

Tom, part of the security team, was now in the process of opening the SUV's other passenger door. Finn did a double take. A dark-haired and dark-skinned boy jumped out of the car. Despite looking Nepalese, the boy was dressed in khaki shorts and a shirt with shoulder lapels, looking like he had been outfitted straight out of a REI Co-op catalogue or an ad for Outback Steakhouse. "Sophie?"

Sophie, shaking her head at Hardy, hurried past Finn and started speaking in a dialect of Punjabi that Finn didn't recognize. She wrapped her arm around the boy's shoulder and squeezed then crooned in a soothing tone. And Finn couldn't look away. This was Sophie, the sensitive child with a generous heart, who was always aware of other's hurt and always wanting to comfort.

Hardy, his open denim shirt blowing in the wind, ambled toward Finn. "Alex Hardy. You're Sophie's childhood friend. She's told me about you and your brothers, you're all American heroes."

Yeah, Finn hoped to hell the guy didn't thank him for his service, because he wasn't sure what his reaction might be. While Finn was in Mexico taking a knife, Hardy was worming his way into Sophie's good graces once again.

"Dude, sorry about showing up unannounced." Hardy pushed the hair escaping from his bun away from his brow, in a well-practiced gesture. "I thought Sophie wasn't leaving Nepal for another week. I just got in from Hong Kong. I'm doing an Asia tour and…"

Finn's bunched muscles and the uptick of his heart rate messaged that his body remained ready for some aggression. Lucky for Hardy Finn was in control, but one punch to Hardy's perfect face would help him relax after his long flight.

Sophie took the boy's hand and came around the back of the SUV. "Finn, I want you to meet my surprise." Her eyes were twinkling in her mischievous way. "Meet Tariq."

Tariq bowed his head.

"*Sat Shri Akaal,*" Finn said. There weren't many benefits of spending time in FATA, the Federally Administered Tribal Areas of Pakistan, the hotbed of terrorists, but seeing the shock on Sophie's face almost made the months of working in the God-forsaken area worthwhile.

Tariq's dark eyes widened when he smiled.

Sophie searched Finn's face. "I didn't know you spoke Punjabi."

"There are loads of things you don't know about me, Soph." Finn didn't mean the words to come out as a sensual promise but by the color extending across Sophie's cheeks, she didn't miss the sexual implication. As a gorgeous woman who had started attracting men's attention early, Sophie knew a come on. She searched Finn's face, her eyes questioning, measuring. God, he was off his game today.

"Where is Uncle Harry?" Tariq asked.

Sophie turned to look at the boy. "When did you start speaking English, Tariq?"

The gangly youth held his two fingers apart. "A little. I practice with Bhikshu Bunan. To get me ready for the trip."

Finn didn't know whether to laugh or swear out loud. Sophie's surprise was bringing this boy back to the States, not marrying Hardy? Finn watched the way Hardy took in Sophie's tender looks toward Tariq. Finn wasn't delusional. Hardy had plans to be part of Sophie's future, but for how long was the question. "We need to get this show on the road."

Sophie gave Finn the evil eye with her forehead furrowed and her eyes narrowed. "Tariq, I'll be right back. Do you want to load your bag on to the plane?"

"Can I speak to you?" Hardy touched Sophie's arm. "I know you're taking off."

Finn stepped between them. "Give me a minute with Sophie, Hardy. And then she's all yours."

Hell, Finn didn't mean it to come out that way.

CHAPTER THREE

"Sophie," Finn growled her name. Damn, the woman already had him on an emotional roller coaster less than three minutes after his feet hit the tarmac.

With all the male eyes tracking them, Finn pulled her aside to avoid being overheard by the inquisitive spectators.

"What the hell, Soph? Surprises are like birthday cakes, showing up when you're not expected, sending a present. Not bringing a Pakistani boy with you to the States."

Sophie jerked her arm out of his grip. "Reeves okayed all of his paperwork."

"Reeves's responsibility is IT. He doesn't make decisions about your safety. I do."

"You used to be entertained by my surprises." Sophie stared into his eyes, as if to read his thoughts. "Remember the time I ordered a monkey for Jordan's birthday? Not that I'm comparing Tariq to a childhood prank."

A gruff laugh erupted out of Finn. "You wanted the monkey for yourself. You loved the *Curious George* books when you were little."

Sophie rolled her eyes affectionately. "Whatever you say, Finn."

And there it was, the shared bond between them flaming into Finn's chest and melting the cold ice that had formed around his frozen heart from the years of violence.

"The look on my father's face when he came home and spotted my mother trying to hide George. And the noise when the monkey shrieked."

Sophie's luminescent eyes softened and Finn wanted to pull her close. "I remember my mother telling my father how industrious it was of me to figure out how to have George delivered as a surprise for Jordan. But it didn't take much skill when Fredrick, our butler, loved helping me play tricks." Fredrick was like all the men who fell under Sophie's spell—willing to do anything to make the spirited girl happy. And Finn, like Fredrick, was sinking fast under the magical spell of the enchantress.

He couldn't let Sophie sway him about this possible dangerous situation. "Sophie, back to Tariq." Finn didn't want to hold his Pakistani background against the boy. But hell, Finn wasn't about to allow a terrorist-in-the-making on the plane with Sophie. She was too innocent to know what being raised on hate for generations did to vulnerable children. For all he knew Tariq could be an Al-Qaeda, Lashkar-e-Omar, Lashkar-e-Taiba, Jaish-e-Mohammed or Sipah-e-Sahaba wannabe, just to name a few options. And those were just the big-name terrorist groups in Pakistan. "Do you know anything about him? His family?"

Sophie stomped closer. "I know you think I'm naïve, but I'm very aware of my father's power and how people want to get close to me because he is rich and famous."

Finn was impressed with his self-control in not mentioning Hardy who appeared on all the tabloids regularly with his newest movie star girlfriend. The man was a hound dog and coming from Finn that was saying a lot.

"Tariq's family was killed in a mosque bombing targeting his Ahmadi religion. But most importantly Bhikshu Bunan wouldn't have asked me if he thought there was any danger." Sophie's face looked hopeful and Finn of all people didn't want to shoot down her relationship with the monk. He could see by the clearness in her eyes and the feistiness in her voice that the time in Nepal had been helpful. When he'd put her on the plane two months earlier, she had looked like the lost teenager she'd been when her mother died. But Finn was supposed to trust a monk who lived in Nepal to understand the risks and dangers of taking a Pakistani boy to the US? The good news by the boy's close-fitting REI outfit, Finn didn't have to pat him down to look for wires.

"Okay, say he does come with us. What then? Is he going to live with you? Are you sure Hardy's up for Tariq as a son?"

"What does Hardy have to do with Tariq?"

A sliver of hope broke through Finn's gloomy mood. He hated that he was damn happy that Sophie didn't catch on. She continued, "He's going to live with his relative's friend on Orcas Island. You'll approve, the man is an ex-Marine who now leads a meditation society for wounded soldiers on the island. I thought you and I could take him to Orcas Island since I have to go to help Jordan plan the wedding."

Finn's heart pitched like heavy sea rollers. Sophie wanted them to share a trip to the place embedded into his being with wonderful recollections of their shared childhood. Her father owned an expansive waterfront property on a beautiful island in the San Juan Islands. His memories of those idyllic summer months with Sophie motivated the work he did—to ensure children the world over had memories of laughter, innocence and adventure, and had helped Finn survive in some of the world's most miserable hell holes.

"I haven't been back to Orcas in years." Finn searched Sophie's face, looking for clues of how she felt. Did she too cling to the memories when surviving got rough? Knowing Sophie's need to be all over his business, she most likely wanted to heal Finn who couldn't hide from her the toll his years of service had taken. Hell, did she know about his latest injury? It didn't matter. Time alone with Sophie... But he was getting ahead of himself.

"Did Bhikshu Bunan give any reason why the boy couldn't stay in Nepal?" This was a disaster in the making.

"Oh, Finn," Sophie placed her hand on his arm and the touch had Finn leaning toward her warmth like a sun deprived plant. "His closest living relative, an uncle who brought him out of Pakistan, died a few months ago. The uncle gave Bhikshu Bunan the name of a man to send Tariq to live with when he died."

Finn, Navy SEAL operator, complete with Uncle Sam's million-dollar intelligence training, said bye-bye to logic and reality. Sophie wanted to help the boy because he was an orphan. Sophie had been like an orphan after her mother died. Her grieving father abandoned his two daughters, withdrawing into his work, ill-equipped to handle his daughters' grief.

"And you've spoken to this Marine? What if, once Tariq gets to the States, this guy doesn't want him? What then?"

Sophie chewed on her plump lower lip. "This is exactly why I didn't tell you." Finn got the subtext—she waited so she could work her magical baby blues on him. And damn, as hardened as he was, he wasn't immune to the effect this woman's tender, caring attitude had on him.

"You've become so cynical. Now you only see the worst in people."

Finn looked down at Sophie's upturned, trusting face. Her thick lashes lifted treating him to the sight of her deeply saturated blue sapphire eyes with flecks of luminescent silver.

"Soph, I'm not cynical." His job guaranteed him to always see the worst to assure his and his team's safety. "I just have a different view from my experience." He didn't add he had seen and done things that no one as sensitive as Sophie should ever know. Sensitive Sophie took everything and everyone to heart, listening, absorbing others' pain. Finn didn't want her to suffer, didn't want to burden her with his battle scars or the danger inherent in his work. Another reason he kept silent about his feelings for the last few years. Sophie deserved better than a brutal frogman, but not a damn self-absorbed musician.

Finn saw Nick point to his watch. Yes, they needed to get this rodeo going, but nothing was ever simple with Sophie. And why did he feel more alive when involved in one of her complications?

"Look, Soph. I get why you want to help this kid, but I'm in charge of your safety. Bottom line he's not going with us until I talk to Reeves and this Marine on Orcas Island."

Sophie's head tilted to the side, her curls brushing over her eye. "Sure, Finn."

Finn blew out a few choice words with blistering heat under his breath as she walked toward Hardy. There was trouble with a capital T. He'd learned never to trust a compliant Sophie.

CHAPTER FOUR

Finn punched numbers into his cell phone as he walked away. Unlike the men Sophie usually hung around, Finn paid little attention to his appearance as evident by his disheveled hair, frayed jeans, faded black t-shirt, and scuffed boots. No designer jeans calculated to look worn and torn or expensive, wind-blown, tussled haircuts held in place by product for Finn. Why should he go to fashionable lengths when he had the confident, male swagger nailed down? He was a walking sex on a stick, and didn't every woman know it? And Sophie had years of watching women pant and beg for that overloaded testosterone.

Familiar with the way he held himself, knowing every gesture of the wild boy she grew up with from the tilt of his head when he was concentrating, to the way his pale eyes lit up when he grinned after one of his practical jokes, to the way he ground his teeth when frustrated—she detected a change.

Something was off in his usual sexy saunter. He was leaning heavily to his left side. His alpha-assertive stride was gone. Had he been injured on his last mission? Knowing the pig-headed man, he'd never admit to being injured, or anything that might resemble a weakness, never even admit to being human.

"You look upset, Sophie, what did he say to you?" Alex startled her out of her absorption with Finn. "I don't take that kind of shit from my security. Remember, he works for your father. You don't have to do what he says."

By how Finn was clenching his phone and his jaw thrust forward, he was giving Reeves a hard time. This was her fault. She wanted to make Finn laugh, find a way back to their close, teasing relationship before the kidnapping, before Finn became tense, on edge around her. "He didn't say anything to upset me. He's just doing his job. And he's an old friend, so it's different than your guys."

"Friend? Are you kidding? The guy's got the hots for you."

Sophie jerked back. No way! Finn never showed interest in her. Sophie grew up watching the parade of women pursue Finn and had seen how he *let* the really blatant ones catch him.

Finn was the reason she went through her bad-boy phase. She wanted to know what she was missing. To experience the sensual promises in Finn's seductive smile, the way his body angled toward the woman in his possessive, domineering way. She wanted to be the focus of all that hot male attention. Sadly, no other boy— or man—had fulfilled her fantasies.

"No. Never." Sophie shook her head. "If anything, Finn's always been in love with my sister." Finn had to be hurting with the loss of Jordan to another man—not just any other man, but a friend Finn had served with. It was serendipitous that Bhikshu Bunan had given her a reason for Finn to accompany her to Orcas Island.

"Sophie, trust me. The territorial vibes were strong and clear. Finn doesn't want me dating you."

"No, he's protective. Always been that way." It had been strained between them after the abduction, but she thought it was her and her hyper-awareness of every little thing around her. Knowing how protective and how committed Finn was, she understood that he was trying to come to grips with his belief that he somehow failed her. And since Finn blamed himself for her abduction, he's gone off the charts to Attila the Hun protector mode. Like the abduction was his fault. Like it was anyone's fault but evil men.

Sophie looked back at Finn who was watching her and Hardy. She smiled not sure what had just happened. Always ready for a quick comeback, all she could do was stare when Finn had told her in that low, warm rumble that she didn't know everything about him. His forceful darkened eyes had been filled with promise, a sensual promise of long nights... She was making the whole episode weird. This was Finn, her childhood best friend.

"Earth to Sophie." Alex nudged her shoulder.

"What?" No. Alex was wrong. It was Finn's guilt making him act differently toward her. Nothing more. Alex didn't know Finn in his take-charge mode like she did. And although she didn't say anything, Alex was lucky that Finn just gave him dirty looks after Alex's stunt of arriving unannounced instead of texting. It wasn't as if Alex didn't understand how security worked.

Alex lifted her chin with one finger. "I want to spend time with you once this tour is finished. Let me come to Seattle, we can take it slow."

"Alex, we've already gone over this. Right now, I need to go home and focus on the summit. And then figure out what I'm going to do next."

She was considering her father's offer of taking over the management of the family's philanthropic foundation named in her mother's honor. It was an olive branch after his years of neglect. Spending time with the refugees in Nepal opened her eyes to the power she had as Richard Dean's daughter to make a difference. It was time to step into the responsibility of her wealth.

"Can't I be what you do next?" Alex raised his eyebrows in mock exaggeration.

Sophie laughed and punched him in the arm. "Nice try, Hardy."

"Seriously, Sophie." Alex brushed away her hair which kept blowing in her eyes from the high winds in the mountains. "I'll need downtime after this tour and I can do that anywhere. Besides I have to be in Seattle for your philanthropy summit."

Sophie touched Alex's hand. He was physically a beautiful man, the kind she was drawn to in her wild days, the kind of man who would be an exciting thrill ride, and maybe after all she had been through, she deserved male attention to help her forget. "If you and I are seen together, the press will go crazy. Wild, rich girl and bad-boy musician. Can you see the headlines?" Sophie was done with making headlines. She wanted to be more than Richard Dean's wild child. "This is about the refugee crisis, and I won't detract or make it about me in any way."

"No one needs to know."

Sophie couldn't suppress the snort. "Yeah, right. No one is going to notice Alex Hardy."

"I just want to spend time hanging out—getting to know each other better. No pressure. We're both at the summit." He leaned closer, pitching his voice into his dark baritone range. "I'm wrapping up Asia in a few days and then I'm coming to Seattle. Will you make time for me, Soph?"

She always did have a weakness for musicians—and their ability to use their voices to seduce. Her sensitive awareness to sound, rhythm of speech, and pitch made her skilled in languages, but vulnerable to bad boys with whiskey-smooth voices. "Let me get through the summit. And then we can see."

"Let's go, Sophie." Not looking happy with whatever Reeves and Jeremy Brophy said to him. Finn marched over still holding himself tight.

"Looks like it's time." Sophie smiled at Alex, ignoring his smoldering stare. He wasn't like her past bad-boy musicians. Alex was using his rock star status to bring attention to the plight of immigrants all over the world. "Take good care of yourself, Alex."

"See you in Seattle." Alex wrapped his arms around her, and whispered into her ear so that Finn couldn't hear. "I'm not giving up. You're the woman I want."

Sophie pulled away and didn't look at either Alex or Finn, merely strode to the plane. Already her determination to take a break from emotional entanglements and bad-boy musicians was weakening before she even left Nepal. But how many women could walk away from Alex Hardy?

She waited at the bottom of the stairs to the plane for Finn to catch up. Since Tariq wasn't in sight, it was obvious he was being entertained by the airplane crew. "You're satisfied with what Reeves and Jeremy Brophy reported about Tariq?"

"Satisfied? Are you kidding? I don't like surprises."

"That's exactly why you should have them." Sophie smirked and climbed the stairs. Taking care of Finn and Tariq were still part of her plan. And she was learning bad boy musicians were easier to handle than sexy, smoldering heroes. One in particular....

CHAPTER FIVE

Finn stretched out on the beige leather loveseat—a far cry from the hard sidewall seats on the military's C-17 fixed aircraft he was used to traveling in—and closed his eyes. And tried to close his mind to the image of the intimate way Sophie touched Hardy and then playfully punched him. Finn stomach churned with gnawing regret.

He slowed his breathing and tried to stop picturing Sophie smiling at Hardy. When Finn felt a nudge against his ribs, he thought he was still dreaming. "Go stretch out on the bed. Tariq crashed on the sofa."

Finn opened his eyes to see Soph's heavily-lashed violet blues peering at him. He had just closed his eyes. "I'm good. Don't need sleep."

"Are you kidding? You've been asleep for two hours."

What? SEALs never slept unaware. Obviously, the combination of lack of sleep, jet lag, and his injury, had knocked him out. No way in hell was he going to get into bed unless Sophie joined him. "I'm fine right here. Tell me when we'll have the pleasure of seeing Hardy again." He really was pissed, exhausted, and off his game, if those were the first words out of his mouth.

"Not exactly sure, though he's speaking at my summit next week."

Finn wasn't looking forward to the international conference that Sophie had organized in Seattle. It was a logistical nightmare for him and his crew. All the Deans would be attending.

"And of course, he wants to spend time with you while he's in Seattle."

"He does. Can you imagine the press?"

Finn kept to himself that the asshole wouldn't want to miss the chance to be spread across *People* magazine with Sophie, gorgeous, sweet and the youngest daughter of the second richest man in the country. Sophie sat across from him, making him draw in his legs, and pull on the damn stitches.

"When were you planning to tell me?"

Finn straightened in his seat unsure if Sophie, who knew him better than anyone, including his brothers and team, had finally figured out how he felt about her.

"You didn't think I'd notice?" Sophie's voice was incredulous.

Finn took a deep breath. "Nothing to worry your pretty, blonde, curly head about, Soph. I can handle it."

He could always get a rise out of her by his condescending comment whenever she snooped into his work or love life.

This time instead of getting all riled, Sophie laughed. "Did you really think I'd fall for that line? Really, Finn, I'm not thirteen any longer. And stop avoiding the question."

"It's classified." He was winging it now.

"What crap!" She had changed into exercise tights and a sweatshirt of some sort that kept falling across her shoulder, causing a burning hunger to run his finger along her slender pale shoulder and then follow the sensual touch with his lips.

"Your injury isn't classified. Another gunshot wound, isn't it?"

He had to hold back a loud hoot of laughter that this questioning wasn't about his earlier slip of exposing his insatiable need for her. "And how do you know what is or isn't classified?"

"Because between your and your brother's adventures, we've always known about the injuries. If you don't tell me, I'm going to call Uncle Harry. Does he know?"

"Soph, you wouldn't call Uncle Harry and worry him for

nothing when's he's in Hawaii for R & R. He's still recovering and you don't want to upset him." Finn and his brothers were helping out in the family security firm while their uncle recovered from a bullet wound to his chest.

"FYI, I spoke with him this morning and he is doing fine."

Hell, did his uncle tell Sophie that Finn demanded to be the one to pick her up? Knowing Sophie, she would have badgered him about it, wanting to know why. And his uncle wouldn't reveal anything since Finn never believed his uncle would approve of Finn, a Navy SEAL, for Sophie. Though Harry was Finn's blood relative, Sophie's happiness would always come first for him. And as his uncle damn well knew SEALs didn't exactly make dependable and stable partners.

"Finn." Sophie leaned forward giving him a stellar view of her abundant cleavage in a red athletic bra down. He shifted in the seat and swore steadily at himself.

"Soph." His voice came out gritty with need.

She raised her eyebrows, crossed her arms over her chest and swung her foot.

He wanted to grab her foot and place in in his lap and see where Sophie's imagination would take her. "I'm fine. I got a few stitches to my stomach. No biggie."

Sophie perused him carefully. She tracked his entire body from his overgrown military haircut to his favorite boots. It was good that SEALs had incredible mastery over their bodies or her baby blues lingering on his stomach and groin would be a problem, a very specific problem that sparked to life with the hope of having her full attention.

"Let me translate Finn speak. You probably have twenty to thirty stitches and it is a big deal."

Despite his intensive training—and practice—in lying under interrogation, he never got anything past this meddling woman. And why did he hope she'd always be meddling in his life? "Soph, all you need to know is that I'm fine. Unless, of course you want to play nurse and examine me?"

Sophie's eyes widened, her forehead furrowed as she tugged on her pillow soft lower lip. "Nice try, Jenkins. I know you'd never let me near you."

Finn couldn't breathe. His heart rate ratcheted up five knots. The way Sophie said it was like a question, not her usually flippant "whatever" tone. Was she hoping for a different answer than his usual? A man could dream.

She brushed away a curl that had fallen out the ponytail she'd pulled her hair into. And Finn couldn't look away from the feminine gesture. Hunger jamming his throat.

"Did someone shoot you or stab you this time?"

He didn't see any purpose in discussing how close he came to bleeding out and how many times he had been close to dying on this last mission. Or the previous ones this past decade and more. Tender and sensitive, Sophie kept him on edge. He didn't want her seeing him as weak, or vulnerable. And to be honest, though he knew he should think of Sophie as a strong, resolute woman—as she'd proved herself during her kidnapping—he didn't want his recollections of potential death and pain to flood her mind. "Not your problem."

Sophie uncrossed her leg and leaned back in the chair, not fooling Finn for a minute on how he hurt her feelings. Her tell was the way her eyes widened and she chewed her lower lip, a habit she'd learned from her heartless bastard of a father. "What did Mr. Brophy say about Tariq? Did he say how he knew Tariq's Uncle Parvez? And isn't it an amazing coincidence that Jeremy Brophy lives on Orcas Island?"

Finn didn't believe in coincidences but he kept his thoughts to himself. He didn't need another talk by Sophie on serendipity and synchronicity.

Sophie leaned forward, her eyes narrowing on his face. "I'm not sure what exactly is going on, but your last mission must have been a doozy." She threw herself back in the seat. "Oops, I forgot. I'm not supposed to mention it. It's classified."

This was another reason Finn hadn't declared his feelings for Sophie. She could never be a military wife, never tolerate all the classified secrets he had to keep. Oh, and Sophie was the daughter of a tech billionaire who was a press magnet. Not exactly a low-profile wife for a Special Forces undercover operator. Finn didn't expect her father would ever approve of Finn's prospects. And Finn never wanted to be the man who married her for money. For all those reasons he'd be hesitant about approaching Sophie. Yet since her kidnapping, he'd been battling all those negatives with the desire to keep her safe in his arms.

"Which is it? How badly you were injured or you don't want to talk about your conversation with Jeremy Brophy?"

"With your skills, you should work for the CIA."

It was hard to describe the way Sophie's forehead bunched together and her shoulders tightened, still he always knew when he'd crossed a line.

"Finn, why are you being more of a jerk than usual?"

Because his wound was aching and the reunion he imagined with Sophie the entire time he was lying in the hospital was playing out with another man touching her, whispering sexy stuff into her ear.

"Look, I'm not trying to hide anything from you. I received great care and I'm on the mend. And talking to Jeremy Brophy went exactly as I expected from Reeves's report. He runs a meditation center and sounds exactly like an Orcas Island kind of guy." Finn didn't share that Brophy's military record was redacted as was what had been doing for five years after his military career.

"Did you get any bad vibes from him, using your secret SEAL interrogation skills? You know he's a good guy?"

"Are you doubting Bhikshu Bunan's judgment?"

"Bunan lives on a mountain in Nepal. I'm not sure if he's ever encountered evil men."

Finn wanted to reach across the small distance between them and pull Sophie on to his lap and reassure her that she'd never deal with bad guys again. Sophie had never discussed the kidnapping after the initial days. He didn't want to upset her with his guilt, and his crazy-ass feelings that had him twisting in knots. He was grateful for his latest spin out because it had let him escape Seattle. Of course, coming back injured wasn't in the plan.

"The dude checks out. And I didn't get any red flags." All the same, Finn was withholding final judgment until he met the man in person. And then he would have to deal with the fallout about Tariq's future if Brophy didn't pass inspection. Though having Sophie's rich, well-connected father would ease the difficulty of finding placement for refugee boy. What Finn would have to deal with was Sophie's feelings. Dealing with pissed off ex- or current Special Forces soldiers was easy for Finn. He did it regularly with his brothers and Uncle Harry. But Sophie...

"There is nothing for you to worry about." And he knew as the words left his mouth, they were going to come back and bite him in the ass.

CHAPTER SIX

Acting as if this day was no different from any other leisurely Sunday watching his stable of ponies compete, Gulam strolled across London's Polo Club grounds, minutes from Hyde Park Corner to meet Asif.

He nodded to a cluster of royals enjoying the sunny September day, their centuries-long passion for horses embedded in their blue blood. As the CEO of a Dubai global import/export company, he was, despite his Pakistani roots, a respected member of the exclusive Polo club, thanks to his donation of hundreds of thousands of pounds.

Asif, as his head of security, knew better than to bring any of his export business to this private bastion. The older man paced in front of the Bentley, pulling a drag from his awful Turkish cigarette.

"Give me one good reason that I shouldn't have you killed for appearing here." Gulam wasn't above killing his favorite relative despite that—or especially since—his cousin looked almost identical to Gulam's older brother with his long, pointed nose and chin and bulky torso. The distinct difference between the two men was Asif's penchant for sadistic violence.

"The trail to find Tariq in the refugee camp was a dead end."

Gulam would have flown to Nepal himself to find his nephew if he weren't required to attend the philanthropy summit in Seattle. His appearance with the richest leaders working on global issues for the poor would help distill the rumors of his shadier business practices. Social media images were vital.

"Why are you really here? This is no different than yesterday's report and every day before that." By the way Asif's shoulders sagged, there was more. More that Gulam wasn't going to like.

"Your sister has disappeared."

The acid burn of betrayal was on his lips, his tongue, searing into his gut. "What of her twenty-four-hour surveillance?"

Asif nervously tugged at the collar of his oxford, blue shirt. "She had an appointment at Mayo hospital in Lahore. Then she decided to shop at Shalmi market. Yasra went into the crowded market, and at some point, must have changed places with another woman, an accomplice, wearing the same hijab. My man followed the wrong woman through the endless rows of the market before realizing the deception."

Pride in his sister's ability to outwit her security guards stirred memories of his mischievous younger sister who never resigned herself to her place in family and society.

"And what of the woman your man followed?" Gulam didn't need to ask about the guard who failed in his duty. Punishment would be meted out for his error. Asif didn't tolerate mistakes when it came to Gulam's family.

"The silly woman maintains she doesn't know Yasra. And it was her usual day to shop. We released her. Just in case, I have a man posted at her house to watch for Yasra."

"Yasra won't come back. And the woman is probably from the mosque." Gulam's family were deeply religious Ahmadi Muslims despite the government of Pakistan declaring the sect heretics and imprisoning any Muslim who identified as Ahmadi.

Gulam exploited the Pakistani's hatred of the Ahmadis for his own rewards. He could care less about the Koran and achieving heavenly peace or he might have mourned the death of his father, brother, sister-in-law, and their daughter, all blown to smithereens five years ago attending daily call to prayer in their mosque.

His nephew was the only survivor, the only one who witnessed Gulam bringing a briefcase into the mosque before the explosion.

Gulam, in his role as the grieving uncle, and head of the family and executor of his family's considerable wealth, brought Tariq into his care. Gulam denied the boy's memory of his presence at the mosque, reassuring him it was all part of his confusion with the traumatic day. As the years went by, Gulam was convinced that Tariq believed the revised story.

Tariq was like his father with a quick wit, amiable disposition, and readiness to forgive. None of the traits Gulam possessed or ever tried to acquire. Why should he compete with his older brother, the focus of his father's love, and the beneficiary of the family wealth?

Asif spit out in disgust. "What kind of Muslim allows his wife to help another escape the protection of her family?"

Yasra wasn't being protected, she was a prisoner. Gulam didn't want to think of what Yasra possibly shared to enlist the help to escape her prestigious and respected brother at the mosque. She had no proof. Tariq was the only proof. To save Tariq's life, she helped the boy escape last year, knowing she, like Tariq, were untouchable, since any more sudden family deaths would raise too many questions.

He wouldn't kill his sister for the latest transgression, but she would be punished. Tariq might not be as fortunate. He had to think of his daughters' future. Tariq was the next heir to the family fortune as the son of the eldest male. The incredible wealth his grandfather had acquired in mining gemstones helped finance Gulam's expansion into the drug trade, including an ephedrine factory in India—necessary for his worldwide distribution of meth.

"Tell me you have a plan to stop her before she leaves the country." Gulam leaned against the vintage Bentley, knowing Asif wasn't fooled by his pose of nonchalance. Yasra was headed to Nepal for Tariq. Knowing how clever his sister was she might hide for months, not wanting to lead him to Tariq.

"She got rid of her cell phone. And because the men were afraid to report her loss, we've lost critical hours in tracking her. She could be anywhere."

"She has been planning this for a while, probably since she helped Tariq disappear." No one except Asif knew that his sister was the one who engineered his nephew's escape into Nepal. It had taken Gulam months to figure out how Tariq vanished, with Yasra pretending ignorance and feigning worry for her nephew. With false tears and concern, she had played him for a fool. Oh, he had made sure she'd suffered for her transgressions.

Despite Asif's intense "questioning," Yasra never confessed how or where Tariq had escaped.

Eventually Gulam's men discovered that an elder from the mosque had taken Tariq to Nepal. Despite the search, Tariq hadn't been found among the wave of refugees.

Gulam was a patient man. He hadn't achieved his success by rushing into circumstances. If Yasra got Tariq out of Nepal into the US with the CIA trying to nail him and his "export business" it would be all over despite his philanthropic image-building.

"I want all our export business clients focused on finding Tariq. Offer a half a million dollars reward."

"To bring him back to Pakistan?"

Gulam shrugged. "Inshallah." As if he believed in Allah's will.

CHAPTER SEVEN

Sophie grabbed the bottle to keep Tariq from dousing his fried oysters like Finn, who had covered his basket of greasy heaven in the hot sauce. Go big or go home was Finn's creed. Except for the one and only spectacular exception, her blonde hair, golden in the sunshine streaming through the large window, seated across from him. He was fearless in everything except for his feelings for this slight woman who had the power to rip his heart out of his chest. Something he realized he'd been repressing far too long.

"Finn, explain to Tariq that he shouldn't copy everything you do, including burning the roof of his mouth with unfamiliar hot sauce."

Although never leaving Sophie's side, Tariq imitated Finn's every gesture including Finn's stride which was comical since Finn was still guarding his gut.

Finn winked at Tariq. "Tariq, the oysters are going to be spicy if you add hot sauce. And you definitely shouldn't do everything I do." Like having a hard-on because Sophie was licking ketchup off her fingers. He felt as immature as Tariq at the moment.

Finn could barely take his eyes off Sophie—the swipes of her pink tongue causing a feverish path to his groin. "Is that what you wanted to me to say, Soph?"

"Finn," Sophie rolled his name from deep in her throat. And sparks ignited to the base of Finn's spine, flooding his body with heat as he imagined Sophie saying his name as he took her to the edge.

Finn averted his stare and dove into his basket of oysters and fries, knowing that Tariq watched every interaction between him and Sophie. Finn had no intention of being outed by a ten-year-old. Talk about not manning up.

"We eat spicy food in Pakistan."

Both Sophie and Finn froze. Tariq never mentioned anything in the two days they had all been together about his home or who he lived with before he came to Nepal. It was driving Sophie mad because she wanted to know everything about the boy, hoping to help him with this next transition. For Sophie's safety, Finn would have liked more insight into the boy's background.

"What's your favorite dish from home, Tariq?" Trying to act nonchalant, Sophie's voice pitched higher as she popped a French fry into her mouth.

"Nihari made with lamb. My aunt..." Tariq reached into his basket and took a big bite of an oyster. "These are good. Did you really come here when you were my age?" Tariq looked at Sophie while wiping his hand across his lips, brushing away the crumbs from the batter.

The kid was either very good at subversion or it was too painful to speak about his home. Finn couldn't decide.

Sophie pushed away the curl flipping across one eye. "Uncle Harry brought us here. My father would have had a fit if he knew."

Finn felt the wistfulness in Sophie's voice for their childhood days as one crazy Brady Bunch with Uncle Harry in charge. Uncle Harry brought Sophie and Jordan to Orcas Island after their mother died, away from their grieving father. Finn, with Nick and Cooper, came along to give their mother a break, allowing her time to deal with just the twins. Harry, an ex-Marine sergeant, treated the Jenkins boys like recruits. The Dean girls were always treated like ladies—at least when Uncle Harry was watching.

"Your father doesn't like oysters?"

Both Sophie and Finn laughed. Richard Dean liked having fresh oysters from Orcas Island flown to Seattle, not stopping at a dive bar. "No, my father loves oysters. He just wouldn't eat them here at Oyster Heaven." As if Richard Dean, tech billionaire, would ever step foot into a place where the waitress called you honey and your feet stuck to the bar floor.

Tariq looked around the ramshackle bar with its long Formica tables, big screen TVs, and brick barbeque and picnic tables outside. It was clean and definitely a hangout for the locals craving fried food, cheap beer, and sports in the farming and fishing community of Conway, population less than one hundred.

"Why? This place is very nice." Tariq gazed between the several giant TV screens. Why is it so empty?"

Business was very slow on the gorgeous, crisp, early October Tuesday afternoon, just the way Finn planned for the trip to Orcas Island. Empty, boring, with nothing going down.

"I think it was pure circumstance that Uncle Harry found this place. When my brothers and I started getting rowdy in the car, he pulled off the highway to find a place where we could let off steam."

Conway was next to the interstate, a prime location since trucks replaced trains in carrying grain and produce to the port of Seattle. The old railroad tracks were smack in the middle of the little town and the Burlington express still sped through transporting oil from British Columbia.

"What time is it, Tariq?" Finn asked knowing how thrilled the boy was with his new watch.

Tariq carefully pulled back his sweater to examine his Apple watch a present from Sophie. "One-thirty."

Not wanting Sophie to know that they were on a schedule since she wanted to reenact their childhood trips for Tariq. Finn still wasn't sure if she was making this trip for his or Tariq's sake. It didn't matter why Sophie wanted the three of them to be together. It gave Finn time with Sophie, and time to be tortured by her closeness and no clear idea of how to break through the boundaries of their established relationship. Unless he just grabbed her fingers right now and sucked the ketchup off.

"I'm always impressed with Uncle Harry's patience when I think about contending with you and your brothers and then Jordie and me."

Uncle Harry's patience? What about his? Sophie appeared to have no clue about Finn's desperation for her, as if they lived in alternative universes. Having Sophie this close, Finn fantasized exploring every rounded curve, dip, and heat in her body while she wanted to explore every farm and seafood stand along the side roads along Puget Sound and the prime farmland of the Skagit Valley.

Despite the family's helicopters and planes, Sophie wanted to sightsee on their way to Orcas Island. Why Sophie wanted to shop for food was beyond Finn. Sophie had never cooked a day in her life. She was a takeout kind of girl.

Sophie was laughing as Tariq added more hot sauce. She looked up and Finn was captivated by the warmth and amusement in her face. Happiness spread through him—waking his deep craving to be locked in her joy. Everything he wanted was across the table. But hell, she was with a famous rock star. She raised her eyebrows in question, never missing any change on his face or shift in his mood. How could she miss how he felt about her? Did she know but was saving him the pain of openly rejecting him? It would be just like her to protect his feelings.

Suppressing the need to reach across the table and grab Sophie and put her to the test, Finn added more hot sauce to his oysters. If his body was flaming like the fires of hell, he might as well burn everywhere. Tariq watched Finn closely, following Finn's idiocy on his next oyster.

"Are you sure about eating that oyster, dude?" Finn leaned back in the rickety chair and watched Sophie's pure amusement as Tariq's face contorted in shock.

Suddenly there was a roar of sound like a Blackhawk landing in front of the Conway tavern. Grabbing his SIG hidden in the waist of his jeans, Finn immediately jumped up to look out the window. A long row of motorcycles rumbled down the middle of the narrow street.

To make sure all the citizens of Conway were aware of their arrival, the trail of bikers revved their bikes shattering the quiet tranquility with nerve-wracking vibrations.

What the hell? Bikers took road trips into farm country and across the North Cascades highway, not into the middle of nowhere. How did they know about the tavern? Because this was the only show in town that served beer! This couldn't be a coincidence. Finn never believed in coincidences.

He needed Sophie out of here now—before the bikers invaded the tavern. Finn pulled out his phone and texted Nick. No one was miked since this was supposed to be a very chill trip. No surprises. No surprises like fifty fucking bikers looking for a little entertainment.

Sophie wasn't aware that Nick, Drew, and Jack, two newly hired ex-Spec Operators, were outside in another SUV since Finn hadn't announced that they had a team for this trip. Before the kidnapping, each Dean sister traveled with one bodyguard; since the kidnapping teams were assigned. And praise the Lord and hallelujah since Finn was going to need help.

Nick would move their car up to the side of the building for a quick exit. No way was Sophie going to walk through the crowd of bikers in front of the restaurant.

Finn looked at Sophie who was speaking fast in the Lahore dialect to Tariq. Finn followed close enough to understand that she was explaining motorcycle gangs. Tariq twisted to catch a glimpse out of the window as more revved their engines in front of the restaurant. A shudder went through the thin boy's body with the loud roar.

Finn threw down two twenties. "Pack up your food. We're heading out."

Sophie's forehead furrowed and her eyes narrowed into her defensive posture.

Finn picked up her plastic basket of food, wrapping the fries and oysters into the red-checked paper. "Move it, Soph. No arguments. We're out of here now."

Tariq's dark eyes widened in fear. Finn reassured Tariq in Punjabi as he pointed to the boy's food and told him to pack it up.

Tariq's hands started to shake, but he did as he was told.

"Finn, there is no need for us to leave. Those bikers won't be interested in us. They'll think we're a family and pay us no mind."

Oh, sure. A smoking hot blonde, a dark-skinned youth, and Finn with his military mojo. Yeah, a real all-American, Disney family blending with the Scandinavian stock in Conway.

Finn grabbed her arm, ready to drag her out before the bikers filled the bar. "Soph, you promised me if we did this road trip that you would cooperate."

For all the clubbing Sophie did, Finn would have thought she understood male tribal mentality. One jackass was going to say something crude about her and her hot little bod and then others would follow and where would that leave Finn against fifty bikers?

"What if they don't like the mix of our family?" Finn knew Tariq understood a lot more English than he let on. He sure hoped the kid didn't get the gist of his words.

Color washed over Sophie's face, then she stood, whispering to Tariq loud enough for Finn to hear that Finn was always worrying and they would eat their food in the car.

Finn was about to remind Sophie that he understood Punjabi when the front door opened. What happened to bikers' posturing, standing in front of their bikes discussing the performance of their hogs before making a move? Shit. Fuck. Holy Fucking Hell. A few other words were on his lips. Before Finn got them out of the bar, Tariq was going to know every swear word in Finn's expansive and creative vocabulary which was saying a lot with four brothers and teams of SEALs.

The bikers were taking over the restaurant, swarming through the front door, the patio doors, and the side doors, blocking all exits. Finn's phone buzzed with a text from Nick. "Honchoes."

Honchoes. Holy mother of holy mother.

CHAPTER EIGHT

"Holy mother of the biggest fuck," Finn repeated and repeated under his breath. Not a biker's club for retired successful businessmen who could afford the price tag of $100,000 for hogs. Honchoes were a 1% gang notorious for methamphetamine drug trade, money laundering, robbery, extortion, firearms, murder, and assault. If that wasn't enough.

What were they doing this far north? Based in Southern California, they transported meth for the CJNG Mexican drug cartel who ran a billion dollar meth trade, the biggest in North America.

Worry about comments on Sophie's bod vanished. Honchoes were the full-meal, *kill you without blinking* criminals and wouldn't hesitate to gut him to get to Sophie. His bowels spasmed as a visceral reminder of how handy these gangbangers were with blades.

If they left now, Finn would have to push their way through the crowd since there was no rear exit. He wasn't going to risk calling any attention to blond bombshell Sophie. Finn pulled on Sophie's arm. "Sit down. We'll finish our meal here and then leave."

"What the fu....frick?" Sophie growled at Finn. Her attempt to clean up her swearing for Tariq's benefit was hysterical. If his body wasn't mainlining adrenaline fueled by the big and mean ugly threat crowding into the puny dive, he'd laugh out loud.

Sophie grabbed Tariq's hand and pulled him to sit by her. Finn saw the sheer panic on her face as a massive bald dude with a red handkerchief wrapped around his forehead walked past their table. The dude with ink was obviously the leader with Honcho in black letters tattooed across the back of his skull, matching "Honcho" written across his black leather jacket. Talk about overkill.

The six-foot-four creep stared at Sophie who stared right back at him. Not that he expected Sophie to back down even though it had to bring up the time she had been kidnapped by a giant Triad gangbanger who planned to rape her.

Why in the hell were the Honchoes out of their territory visiting Conway, Washington, on a fricking Tuesday? Probably the gangbangers, like Finn, wanted to avoid attention while they moved meth down the coast from Vancouver. Loads of drugs moved between Seattle and Vancouver.

"Keep eating and once they all get settled, we'll go out the side door."

Finn texted Nick to pull up at the side door and for Drew and Jack to retrieve Finn's car.

Finn always sat with the ability to see all egresses and was glad for that entrenched training. He watched as the intimidating Hispanic and Native American gang members trailed in. Laughing and swaggering by their position in the membership. What was it about bikers? Did they all have to be big dudes with badass 'tude— "I've got a chip on my shoulder the size of Rhode Island, and I want you to try to dislodge it"?

It was easy to tell who the officers were since each dude had his name, and his rank on his jacket. Sergeant Gonzalez yelled out they would be staying half-an-hour. Finn's initial reaction was right on. It was better if he didn't take Sophie and Tariq out but instead wait for the Honchoes to leave.

As the men sauntered by, Finn felt every flinch coursing through Sophie's body, every panicked intake of breath. He reached across the table and took Sophie's hand. "It's going to be okay. You trust me, don't you, Soph?"

Finn rubbed his thumb along her cold hand, trying to reassure her and take away any memory she had dredged up.

Sophie snorted. "Trust you? Are you kidding? Trouble follows you, Finn Jenkins."

Now Finn did laugh out loud. Just like Sophie to quote his mother despite being freaking terrified.

"You know you've taken that out of context. My mother says that to every one of her sons. Not just me."

Sophie was about to explain to Tariq when Finn squeezed Sophie's hand. "Might be better not to draw any attention."

Sophie nodded, saying to Tariq in English. "We'll leave soon."

Finn kept smiling and nodding at Sophie and Tariq but never stopped observing the leader and the men gathered around him. If anything was going down, it would happen with these men. Tension prickled Finn's spine. He could almost smell the threat with the sudden shift in the gang's jovial mood. The takeover of the tavern with "aren't we the biggest dicks in town" changed to a silent, tense undercurrent. The little hairs on Finn's neck stood straight up. The tavern went deadly silent.

"Soph, listen to me," Finn leaned forward, closing the distance so they wouldn't be overheard. "I want you and Tariq to move to the side door." Sophie's pupils dilated wide with anxiety. God, how he didn't want any stress for Soph. How did this day become a walking nightmare?

Keeping his voice quiet and even, he said, "Hold onto Tariq's hand, chatting and smiling as if nothing is wrong. Nick is parked right outside the door. And keep moving no matter what you hear. Do you understand me?"

"Finn, you're scaring me. What's wrong?"

"Nothing's wrong, but I want you and Tariq out of here. Now. Go Soph."

Finn hated the way Soph chewed her lower lip but stood and whispered to Tariq, smiling and holding onto the boy's hand while they walked toward the side door. He knew she'd do anything to protect Tariq.

Finn stood up, his hand on his SIG, still tucked in his jeans and followed closely behind. He had no choice but to have his back to a few of the assholes; all the while though, he kept his glare on the leader.

Finn heard the SUV car doors and could see Nick piling Soph and Tariq into the back seat. A "homie" covered in ink showed the leader his phone and pointed to Finn. The leader barked, "Don't let them leave."

Finn took the last two steps out of the bar and shouted as he jumped into the front seat of the SUV. "Let's get the hell away from Conway."

CHAPTER NINE

With tires squealing, Nick peeled away, veering toward the highway with a sharp right. Finn had his SIG out while he reached into the glove box for the automatic SIG Rattler now stashed in the Dean's fleet of bullet-proof SUVs. Never going to be unprepared. Nick's Glock 19M lay ready across his lap.

"Finn, what is going on?" Sophie leaned into the front seat. "How did Nick get here?"

Finn shook his head. He wished to hell he knew the reason the Honchoes were following them. "I don't know, but these guys... Get on the floor with Tariq."

"You're kidding? You want me to lie on the floor while we're driving?" Finn heard the terror in her voice, still there was nothing he could do at this point but protect them from whatever the assholes threw at them.

Nick barked, "Get down, Sophie. Now." Sophie, always intimated by Nick's steely control, immediately complied.

"Did they recognize me?" There was something bleak and awful in her voice.

"Those lowlifes? No way. But we're not taking any chances." Drug runners for CJNG cartel. The same cartel from which Finn had taken out one of their lieutenants in his last mission. One hell of coincidence.

Finn was most likely the target. How in the hell did they get his identity? They were looking at their phones when everything changed in the tavern. The US Navy went to great lengths to protect his identity as a secret operator. He was supposed to be undercover with his identity kept as tight as NSA's website, a G-14 classified government secret.

Tariq shrilled, "They want me, don't they?"

"No, Tariq. This has nothing to do with you." Sophie voice trembled. "Don't worry. Finn and Nick will protect us. Won't you, Finn?"

"Nothing is going to happen to either of you." Rage seized his throat. Finn would die trying before he let a Honcho get near Sophie.

Nick sped onto the long, curvy entrance to 1-5 South. Drew and Jack followed close behind, then crossed the bridge to merge onto 1-5 North. The plan was to force the bikers to divide to chase their quarry. Finn hoped the diversion would help their chances against the fifty-to-four ratio.

A roar came next to Finn's window. "One on your right." The leader drove next to Finn, right at his window. The asshole didn't care that it was a winding narrow merge lane. The bald goon reached into the back of his pants. Finn mouthed, "Good luck with that, asswipe."

The leader grinned and leveled his Glock right at the window. The glass shattered causing spiderweb cracks down the window on Finn's side, but the 9mm slug didn't penetrate. On the attack side, the glass shattered as it was designed to do spraying glass into the air and into the face of the leader. Too bad the asswipe's helmet had the visor down. Still, the dude had to have received a mouth-full of minuscule glass shards. Finn would have smiled at the asshole if he weren't so violently pissed for scaring Sophie and Tariq.

"Finn, please tell me that the bikers aren't shooting at us."

"Soph, we're in a bulletproof SUV. They can shoot at us all day." Finn didn't want to say except for an RPG the SUV was impenetrable. But the good news in this goat fuck situation was that the Honchoes weren't planning the attack in advance so they didn't come with their full arsenal.

Richard Dean could afford military-grade protection. The bulletproof glass would hold. But, for frightening Sophie and Tariq, Finn was tempted to shoot the goon off his bike into never-never land. Except today's mission was to protect, not engage in a gun fight.

Nick shouted and swerved fast and hard to the right. "Got the fucker." The leader slammed on the brakes to avoid flipping out.

"One down, another twenty-four assholes to go," Finn whispered under his breath to Nick, not wanting Sophie to hear. "Looks like they took the bait. Half of them are following Drew and Jack."

On their road hogs, the bikers hugged the curves easily outmaneuvering the heavy SUV. The bikers gained quickly by accelerating on the curves. Would they figure out to aim for the tires? Even the newest Kevlar tires couldn't hold out forever against twenty-four guns.

"Finn, why didn't you tell me you were expecting trouble?"

"I wasn't expecting anything, Sophie." As if...anyone including a paranoid, always prepared Navy SEAL would expect this disaster. Finn kept checking both mirrors. He messed up by wanting to make Sophie happy. He must be on a CJNG hit list and one of the members recognized him. He vowed to protect Sophie diligently, with his life but his work put Sophie straight into the crosshairs of the most vicious drug cartel in North America—the biggest reason he and Sophie could never be together.

Five bikers sped up on Nick's side and kept accelerating next to the SUV, trying to look inside. Nick hit his brakes and the bikers sped right past them.

Nick chuckled. His brother was enjoying the action, after the boring security stuff he'd done since being invalided out of the Marines.

Two bikers came up fast, leaning over their bikes, determined to cut off the SUV. "Two on your right, Nick." The sound of their gunfire ricocheted in the silent SUV.

Finn shouted, "Hold on, Soph and Tariq."

Nick hit the gas and swerved viciously in front of the two bikers. The sudden fast twist jolted the SUV to veer off the highway. With a hard turn on the wheel, Nick righted them onto the pavement. One biker veered to avoid Nick, crashing right into his buddy next to him. They both spun out. The first guy hit the ditch and careened out of control in the grass. His buddy wasn't as lucky, he spun before his bike flipped, throwing him on to the road with the bike on top.

How long could they play chicken with these gangbangers? Finn blew out an exhale of relief with the sound of sirens. One state patrol car sped north past them. WTF? The guy was going after the wrong car. The Honchoes didn't want Drew or Jack. They wanted Finn.

He had endangered Sophie, a young boy, and his brother. Finn hit speed dial for Reeves. "Where the fuck is our backup?"

"Language, Finn," Sophie chimed from her position on the floor.

"Right on, Soph. Finn, keep your act clean." Nick grinned as he swung the SUV between the innocent drivers making their way on the freeway. The Honchoes were still bunched up behind them, rethinking their next attack.

A strange combustible mix of rage and worry rocketed through him. If he didn't have two innocents in the SUV, he wouldn't fleeing those losers but hurting them...

On each side, a biker pulled next to the SUV while the others held back. The bald leader who had gone off the road was back on Finn's side. He smiled, a toothless grin, as he fired rapidly at the tires. That's what Finn always loved about lowlifes—their solution to any problem—just to shoot the hell out of it. Imbeciles. And then what—kill Finn in cold blood on the highway? Most likely, if the reward was big enough. And a Navy SEAL working with the *Mexican Commandos* was definitely a big prize for the drug cartel.

"They're shooting out the tires," Sophie screamed.

"Stay down, Sophie. The tires are bullet proof, but hold onto the kid. It's going to get bumpy," Finn warned in anticipation of Nick's next ballsy move.

Nick veered the vehicle, causing the guy on Nick's side to swerve before slamming into the side of the SUV. Nick accelerated—

adjusting for the impact, drove straight onto the median strip. It was a grassy slope and the rough dips in the knoll threw all of them into the air. Nick slammed the brakes to slow the impact, still Soph and Tariq were tossed into the air.

State troopers swarmed the freeway. And a helicopter above. Praise the Lord. The cavalry had arrived. The Honchoes fast-tracked as a group, whizzing south. Two patrol cars sped after them.

Finn jumped out of the SUV as did Nick. Finn threw open the back door. Tariq was holding onto Sophie's arms as they both struggled to get off the floor. Both were shaking but no sight of blood or obvious injuries. Just scared shitless. "Are you two okay?"

Finn bent and lifted Tariq out of the SUV and set him on the ground.

Drew and Jack came speeding into the median and within seconds were positioned behind the SUV in a protective stance.

Nick joined Finn and put his massive arm around Tariq's shoulder. "You're safe, Tariq. The bad guys are gone." Nick pointed down the freeway where the helicopter and police were chasing the bikers.

Sophie, wedged in between the seats, squirmed to get out. She had taken the brunt of the impact. Finn lifted her into his arms and Sophie fell against his chest. He didn't care, he wrapped her tightly in his arms, squeezing her against his pounding heart. "Finn," her voice barely audible. Her lips constricted into a pale line. "I thought they were going to take me again."

Still holding her in the air, Finn brushed her hair away from her eyes. He had to see her eyes, to make it all better. Her pupils dilated wide like saucers, her shattered face cold and colorless. He never wanted evil to touch her again.

"I'll die before I'll let anyone hurt you." And he kissed her, pouring all his desperate feelings and emotions into the kiss. His mouth crushed down on her cold lifeless lips. He kissed her like he owned her soul and would accept nothing less. She was everything. All he had ever dreamed. All the adrenaline of the chase poured into this kiss, his desperate hunger for this woman. Finn couldn't stop. Didn't care. Her body tightened in shock before her softness melted against him, her body clinging to his.

Nick shouted, "Finn, stop mauling Sophie."

Finn dropped his hands away as if she was an IED about to detonate. Finn, mighty Navy SEAL, lost his focus, his ability to compartmentalize. He pulled back waiting for Sophie to smack him across the face. She gaped at him, her crystalline blue eyes wide, her lips red and swollen from his demanding kiss which gave him territorial satisfaction. She touched her finger to her lips. And, though never lost for words, a shocked Sophie just stared at Finn.

Finn wanted to pull her back into his arms. This was not the place or time though. It was a selfish move on his part to kiss her, to claim her, but it was the one time he'd lost his highly trained control. Only one time after all the endless dreary years. Engaging with the Honchoes brought up all his suppressed fears of losing Sophie, his soulmate, his missing rib—*only when you find the woman of your life will you no longer feel the lingering ache in your heart.* Finn no longer felt the lingering ache.

"We need to make tracks back to HQ," Finn said to Nick who was bent over the SUV, checking the tires.

A lone state overweight trooper, looking not too happy as he climbed out of his car, put his hat on his head and with his hand on his holstered gun on his hip, marched toward the troublemakers Finn and Nick. Finn gave Drew the high sign to handle the trooper. Drew, a big, mean, ex-Army Ranger, stepped in front of the trooper. The poor trooper didn't stand a chance.

"We need to take the other SUV," Finn said to Nick, ignoring the biggest and best mistake he had ever made.

"I'll get the keys from Jack."

Switching to Punjabi, Finn avoided looking at Sophie, afraid of what he might see. The fearless Team Leader of Bravo SEAL team was afraid. He wasn't sure which would be worse, her hurt feelings or rejection. "We're going to go to Uncle Harry's offices where there will be no bad guys. And then we'll get you to Orcas Island."

"But..." Sophie started, Finn shook his head when Tariq turned toward Sophie.

Sophie's eyes narrowed but she restrained herself from asking any questions. There was going to be hell to pay once they were away from Tariq.

"We're going in the other SUV." Finn pointed.

Sophie wrapped her arm around Tariq's shoulder as she reassured him that he was safe. Together they moved toward the SUV as if nothing out of the ordinary had happened. Sophie was solid. She'd do anything to reassure the young boy.

"You're slipping, little bro," Nick taunted Finn despite the fact that they were the same size, Finn would always be the little guy in the Jenkins's pecking order, except, of course, for the twins who were younger than Finn. "Needing a car chase to claim the woman you've wanted for how long now?"

No way was Finn going to admit since he was twenty-three, home from BUD/S training, to see Sophie, the wounded adolescent, who had blossomed into a fearless, gorgeous woman. "Tired after our little chase, old man? Want me to drive?"

"Nice try." Nick chuckled as he climbed into the driver's seat.

Finn was replaying all the mistakes he made today with Sophie and Tariq. The list was longer than any other mission. And the biggest was kissing Sophie out of a need to claim her before the CJNG came after him.

Nick shrugged toward the two overweight troopers who were questioning Drew and Jack.

"Let them handle the troopers. We've bigger fish…"

CHAPTER TEN

Reeves jumped up from his IT command control in the security office and swept Sophie into his muscular arms. "Honchoes? Really? Thought you were done with bad boys?"

Sophie punched him in his formidable six-pack. Immediately her fist stung from the impact with the rock-solid wall; still delivering the punch made her feel a hell of a lot better after the frustrating last few hours beginning with shooting bikers and ending with Finn turning aloof and silent.

The buff IT genius sucked in his gut and bent over dramatically as if her punch impacted his tight abs. "The Honchoes have more ink and piercings than any of your musician boyfriends."

A total-body shiver went through Sophie as she compared the similarities of this gang to the Triad. She wouldn't soon forget the tattoo engraved across the back of the skull of the Honcho leader. "I'm done with bad boys."

Reeves waggled his dark eyebrows. "Alex Hardy isn't a bad boy?"

She should have known. Reeves already was all over her business. "Alex is a humanitarian. Philanthropist. Political activist." Sophie wasn't going to argue about Alex's past reputation. Like Sophie, he was changing his ways, trying to make a difference in the world.

"Hound dog." Finn, Special Forces operator, with amazing skills, could also hear conversations across the massive room while searching through his desk. He had escorted her and Tariq from the underground garage on full commando as though the Honchoes could reappear despite Nick's reassurance that they were gone.

She should be relieved Finn was finally talking to her. Since the scorching kiss, he had shut her out. Like she was the one with the problem. Finn, her best friend, had just changed their entire relationship and then walked away. Why had he kissed her? She didn't believe that Finn, bold macho SEAL, lost control from fighting the bad guys or suddenly developed unquenchable lust for the girl who plagued him his entire life.

"And you must be Tariq." Reeves raised a high-five.

Tariq jumped to hit Reeves's hand and then laughed.

"Guess it takes one hound dog to know another hound dog," Sophie yelled at Finn's back as he crossed to the huge cabinet across the room. He hadn't spoken to her or explained anything about the reason a motorcycle gang shot at them. He was acting so out of character. One minute her BFF, then sexy come-ons, and now obnoxious as hell. Did he suffer more than a physical injury on his last mission? Something was really wrong. She planned to find out.

Reeves draped his arm over her shoulder. "Can you repeat that fast three times?"

"Do you have news of the Honchoes, Reeves?" Finn spoke over his shoulder as he pulled a box down from a shelf.

Looking up at Reeves, Tariq tugged on Sophie's arm and asked in Punjabi, "Is he your intended?"

Finn slammed the cabinet door after pulling a phone out of the box. As he strode toward the conference room, he punched numbers and began speaking in rapid Punjabi, "It's hard to keep track of all of them, Tariq."

Anger rocketed through Sophie. White spots whirled before her eyes. That was it. Finn, the man who changed women as often as Sophie changed her purses had the nerve to comment about her past. She marched toward the jerk. "Finn, I need a word with you. Now."

Seething, she smiled back at Tariq, not wanting to upset him. She'd kept it together for the hour-long ride back from Conway for

Tariq's sake. It was time to have it out. What was going on with him? He had done a great job protecting her and Tariq. She had been frightened. Only an idiot wouldn't be, but not many had Finn Jenkins as a protector. Then he kissed her with a desperate hunger that kept her stomach churning. Sophie touched her lips. The feel of Finn's demanding kiss and his voracious need were imprinted on her body and soul.

"The Honchoes are in custody. Lawyering up." Reeves was guiding Tariq to his gaming station near his desk.

"Where are Sten and Lars? I told them to be here." Finn continued to ignore her on his way down the long hallway to the main conference room.

Sophie followed but Finn was faster.

"They're five minutes out."

"Finn." Sophie wasn't stopping. She ran and grabbed the back of his shirt, fisting her hands in his t-shirt.

"What?" Finn halted and turned, giving her his best impatient *whatever* pose, his arms crossed over his chest, his impressive biceps bulging under his shirt, his fierce jaw locked tight. And Sophie wished her heart didn't flutter suddenly in feminine interest...for Finn. What the hell? Maybe she was suffering from latent PTSD. Jordan, her MD sister, reassured Sophie her flashbacks and nightmares were a normal reaction and would get better with time. All the same, this heightened awareness of Finn was pushing her into a new level of weird craziness.

"I have to make calls. Like the one to your father."

The mention of her father cut short her female fantasies. She hadn't thought about her father's reaction. She had been dreading the call to Jordan, but her father was going to freak out. Not in the normal way, but as only a famous, billionaire, security-geek father would with everything and everyone on speed dial.

After the kidnapping, her father had doubled down on security. Now her security would triple. Jordan thought their father was consulting with NSA about having their satellites track his daughters' whereabouts. Sophie wouldn't put that past her hardwired father.

"I'll call my father. He should hear about today from me. Please don't call Uncle Harry. He's still recovering, and, I don't want him to worry."

"Nick already called Uncle Harry. And wait to call your father. I need more information before I talk to him."

"What sort of information? God, my dad is going to have a SWAT team following me when he hears. And Jordan's going to be hurt that I haven't called her like two hours ago." There went her plan of a low-key return with a relaxing time on Orcas Island supporting her sister's wedding plans. And why did Sophie feel like she had messed up again?

"Please, Soph?" Finn's pale blue eyes had darkened to slate. Was this some sort of trick? Finn asking for help. He was always two steps ahead of her.

She tried to harden herself against those enigmatic, incandescence eyes and the low rumble of his sexy voice. "I mean it, Finn. You're going to tell me."

"Let me get a handle on this and then I'll explain as much as I can."

"Who do you need to call?"

He opened the door to a conference room. "I need to check in with my CO before I talk with your father."

"CO?"

"Commanding officer," Nick answered. Sophie didn't hear Nick come up from behind her.

"Why would… What does your CO have to do with motorcycle gangs?" She pushed closer to Finn to prevent him from brushing her off.

"I'll explain later." Finn closed the door in her face.

Nick took her elbow and steered her away from the door. "I know this afternoon was really upsetting, but we'll get a handle on it soon."

This was the mother lode if Nick, the scary, silent brother, was trying to be reassuring. Anyone who didn't know the Jenkins brothers would have missed the barely perceptible shared look between Nick and Finn before Finn closed the door.

Why would Finn need to talk to his commanding officer? Ideas flashed through her brain. Finn had been injured on his last mission which meant... She wasn't sure what it meant. Finn was always fighting bad guys. His face and arms were tanner than when he left. But he was based in San Diego which got a lot more sun than Seattle. A cold seeped deep into her bones. Biker gangs were often associated with drug cartels like the Triad or the ones in Mexico.

Finn could never tell her about the connection to his last mission and a motorcycle gang but she'd figure it out. She needed Reeves to give her information about the Honchoes.

"The bikers were after Finn, weren't they? Nick, you have to protect him. My father will do everything to stop them."

Suddenly she felt selfish for wanting Finn to go to Orcas Island with her and Tariq.

"Soph, you don't need to worry about Finn. He can take care of himself. Finn will tell us what he can once he gets squared away."

Just because she was little Sophie to Nick and his brothers didn't mean that she wasn't getting involved. She pasted on her best good-girl smile. "Of course, I can wait but we need to call Jeremy Brophy on Orcas Island. He's expecting Tariq."

"One step at a time. Let's wait for Finn."

Sophie was about to ask more questions, then the Jenkins twins arrived. She was never sure when the brothers would surface since they were all in the military. No one ever mentioned Cooper, the second oldest brother, which in the Jenkins brothers' world meant that he was on a secret mission somewhere, doing something that no one would ever know.

"Hey, little man, you're Tariq?" Lars, with the same self-confident swagger as Finn, came into the room with Sten trailing behind him. Lars leaned over the desk where Reeves was demonstrating to Tariq his video gaming area. "Reeves teaching you how to play Minecraft?"

"No violent games, Reeves," Sophie intoned. And how ironic. After witnessing Finn be more of a badass than any avatar conqueror, she didn't want Tariq to play violent games. Of course, his hero worship of Finn's macho attitude of bullets don't hurt me had Tariq watching Finn in mouth open-total awe.

Lars spoke rapidly in Punjabi to Tariq, instructing Tariq to ignore Sten since he was an idiot.

"What are you saying about me?" Sten grabbed Lars's arm. "Did he say that I'm younger?"

Tariq's head was bouncing between the brothers. Sophie rushed to intervene. On a regular day the twins were hard to take but, after the stressful day Tariq had, he didn't need their antics. Sten twisted Lars's arm behind his back and demanded that he beg. Which had both Tariq and Reeves cracking up.

Men. After growing up with the Jenkins boys, she should have expected that, like Reeves, they'd clown around making light of all the danger. Smiling at how Tariq's dark eyes lightened with his wide grin, she now was really dreading calling her sister and father. Unlike these jokers, they were not going to find anything funny about today's car chase and gun battle.

CHAPTER ELEVEN

Finn controlled the urge to punch his fist through the closed door. He was absolutely, positively, royally screwed. The painful pressure building in his chest, seeping into his veins, left him feeling as untethered as when his dad, a fierce Marine, was killed in Desert Storm.

He mastered control of his body and mind to never feel helpless...until two months ago when Sophie had been kidnapped. His life, his career, was orchestrated, rehearsed, total control. And now...he was stuck again in his worst nightmare.

Sophie might fool Nick with her wide-eyed questions, but not him. She would be relentless in getting answers. He had none. And she wouldn't cease until she was caught right smack in the middle of the threat. Finn snapped his jaw back and forth trying to relieve the tension.

Never mind that he had no plausible excuse for the kiss; that didn't stop him from wanting to kiss her again in the middle of HQ. Flashing on how soft her lips were and how she melted for him, her hot little bod molded against him...for a second, he forgot everything like the minor hiccup that he was on the CJNG Cartel's hit list. He ground his teeth together. Royally. Fucked. From all sides. Daddy Dean and Jordan would hold him responsible for endangering Sophie. And they were right.

Falling back on his well-honed SEAL discipline of *the only easy day was yesterday*, he punched the number of Todd

Lancaster, the DEA liaison for the mission in Jalisco, Mexico into a burner phone. Lancaster would be the first to know if CJNG were after Finn. And if they weren't after Finn, he had to consider the possibility that Sophie was the target. He drew in a jagged breath.

Not having a moral compass didn't mean the lowlifes weren't smart and organized. And if they were running meth up the coast, they wouldn't want to draw police attention by suddenly deciding to kidnap the daughter of one of the wealthiest men in the world.

Lancaster picked up after one ring. "Lancaster here."

"Finn Jenkins."

"Ready for another trip to Jalisco? Restless for the action?"

Finn suppressed the need for a four-letter retort. He was back in action. Not by choice. He was supposed to be relaxing on Orcas Island with Sophie.

"My cover might have been blown."

The long pause from Lancaster was never a good sign. The whip-thin guy never stopped moving. As if he mainlined crank, he talked fast, chomped hard on gum, and had the face of a tenacious badger. "No way. That's impossible."

"I ran into the Honchoes in a tavern in Northern Washington. It was a random. Once they checked their phones, the chase was on with the leader trying to blast me with his M40."

"No shit? You running a mission? I thought you were still on the disabled list."

Lancaster was fishing. This was the problem with the work they did. You never believed anyone and never took anything they said as the whole truth.

"No mission. Just an innocent bystander."

"Right."

Finn heard the disbelief. "I didn't know that the Honchoes were transporting that far north."

"Are you sure they made you? Maybe they were after your companions?"

Finn wasn't about to mention Sophie.

"Nope. No connection." Despite Sophie's millions, a dead Navy SEAL was worth more.

He had re-hashed every possible reason for the Honchoes' attack during the tortuous hour-long ride back to HQ. He could hear every impatient intake of Sophie's breath, her heated stare on the back of his neck. She restrained questioning him only because of Tariq. The only logical conclusion was the CJNG were coming for him.

"You're telling me that those Jalisco slime infiltrated the security of the United States Navy?"

Finn had shared in his debrief his concern that the Mexican mission was a setup. Was there someone dirty in the Navy who had access to his file? It was above his pay grade to delve into the operation.

"Not sure." His CO wanted to hear the DEA's assessment of the attack before starting an investigation. The Navy's jurisdiction didn't include biker gangs and their connections to drug cartels. This was the thankless, never-ending job of the DEA.

"Is it possible it's someone on your end?" Finn asked. A long silence stretched for a wired guy like Lancaster. Stories were rampant about DEA agents who went to the dark side, fed up with the hazardous work at low pay.

"Not that I know of." Lancaster's gum chomping boomed over the phone. "Causalities?"

"None. And the gang is in custody."

"Why haven't I been contacted by the DEA office in Seattle about their arrests? They're out of San Diego."

Lancaster was assigned to the San Diego office, but his focus was on Mexican drug cartels rather than the homegrown drug dealers.

"I'm sure you'll hear. They were just arrested."

Finn checked his watch. It had been only four hours since they set out. He gripped the phone tighter as he thought of Sophie's and Tariq's excitement for the road trip.

Lancaster blew out an exasperated breath. "Without anyone dead, they'll be out before you know it. They have powerful connections and high-priced attorneys."

Finn knew how sleaze ran. "I need you to find out if there has been a price put on my head."

"Coming after American military in the US is a risky business even for CJNG. But you did kill El Sencho's first lieutenant. He's not going to forget."

The drug cartels thrived by keeping a tight stranglehold with fear of retaliation. That primitive eye-for-an-eye mentality that kept everyone in their place.

"I'll put feelers out. My deeply embedded guys don't check in unless something big is going down. Do you need protection? Safe house for your companions?"

"I've got the protection covered." Uncle Harry was already covering his mother's safety. He could trust Uncle Harry to not tell his mother the real reason for her heightened security. His brothers could handle themselves, Sophie, however, was another matter. She would never accept being held in a safe house without a credible explanation.

"Until I confirm, you might want to take a longer R & R. Disappear."

"That was the damn plan before Honchoes start shooting at me."

Finn listened but his mind was already focused on his next phone call. He had another month of leave which he had planned to spend his time convincing Sophie they were meant for each other. Would his CO call him back to California because of the threat? He wasn't about to leave Sophie.

"Did they make your companions?"

"Not sure."

"I wouldn't take a chance. The CJNG's reach is long."

Yeah, that's what Finn was worried about. They would retaliate mercilessly against anyone close to him.

"The Seattle office can give you protection. I can make the calls."

Finn wasn't bringing on any DEA agents. He trusted no one other than his own team with Sophie's safety.

"Thanks, I've got it covered. Going to head to an island." The plan clicked into place while listening to Lancaster's dire warnings. Taking Sophie and Tariq off the grid to a secure location on Orcas Island, away from cartel, was the solution. Resuming their trip wouldn't require giving Sophie any answers to the hard questions. And it would give the DEA and the Navy time to sort out the risk.

"An island? Not sure that's such a great idea. Too many risks for exposure and not enough exits on an island."

Not at Richard Dean's fortress. And strangers stuck out on Orcas Island. Drug cartel members would definitely stand out on the island renowned for its organic, laid-back life. And it would take a while for cartel to make the connection between him and the Deans. Or possibly never with the Deans' high level of security and the Navy's practice of keeping the identity of SEALs down low.

"I know you're a SEAL but you're not used to hiding out in your home territory. If you've been made, they'll look at your house, your family. Change out everything."

"Thanks for the heads up." Lancaster didn't know that Finn grew up in the security business.

"How are you getting to this island? They'll be running your name for flights."

"Going to fly out on a private jet. The island has spotty service. I'll have to check in with you. And thanks for all the help."

"I'll get back as soon as I hear anything."

Finn clicked off. One phone call down. And two to go. He wasn't sure which he dreaded more—his CO or Richard Dean, both men who weren't used to having their plans thwarted. And Finn was about to make their days suck.

Yet, facing Sophie, spinning the story to convince her to go to Orcas Island without her realizing the threat, made the phone calls look like child's play. He was a frogman. Time to man up.

CHAPTER TWELVE

Sophie checked and rechecked her phone. She'd give Finn five more minutes. She wouldn't be thwarted by her father's or Finn's overprotectiveness. She deserved a say in the deliberations about her safety going on behind closed doors. Controlling men didn't get to be the sole-decision makers for their loved ones.

She would have already stormed the door, but she didn't want Tariq to witness the battle with Nick. Positioned by the door, Nick's nonchalant act of scrolling through his phone didn't fool her for a minute. He was there to stop her from busting in on Finn.

How long did it take Finn to make phone calls? Uncle Harry, her father and her sister had all called her while Finn was sequestered behind the closed door. Was his CO demanding that he return to San Diego to fight the drug cartel while he was still injured? Reeves said Finn was still on leave for at least a month because of his stab wound.

Nick stood when Finn emerged and they talked in low voices. Whatever Finn said had both of them looking up and staring at her. No matter how many Jenkins men tried intimidate her, she wasn't going to move in with her father away from Finn while he was in danger. Nope. And if they tried, Tariq would see a Sophie he had never experienced.

Sophie marched straight over. No waiting for the men to rule. No giving the Jenkins boys any more time to conspire against her.

"Finn, I'm not moving in with my father. No matter what you and Nick think you can do."

"I told you not to call your father before I spoke with him." Finn spoke in a calm and even voice. Why did he always have to act in command of his feelings while she stewed over his safety and the sizzling kiss that kept her touching her lips at odd moments, beguiled by the softness of his lips and the thrill of his possessiveness.

"I didn't call him. Uncle Harry did. Uncle Harry is leaving Hawaii. I tried to convince him that you could handle whatever or whomever was behind this this afternoon but he wouldn't listen." Sophie was secretly pleased that Uncle Harry was coming home to protect Finn. Not that Finn would ever admit that he needed help. "And my dad is adamant that I move back into his fortress."

Sophie and her father were making progress in their fractured relationship but not enough to sustain a move back home to the fifteen-bedroom mansion with the latest in security tech, including guests being microchipped when visiting. Her father, who'd shut down completely after their mother died, was trying to make amends with his daughters after their abduction. She wasn't ready to go back to the family home that held painful memories from her very lonely adolescence.

"I'm going to Orcas Island. The house is totally secure. Jordan is so upset and is insisting that Aiden be my personal bodyguard. I'm not having Aiden watching me 24/7. It would be too bizarre." Jordan's fiancé was a good guy for a six-foot-four Special Forces guy who radiated an *I-can-kill-you-in-ten-seconds* mojo.

Sophie was betting her last million that Finn would never agree to Aiden guarding her. Finn stood with his legs apart, his arms crossed over his broad chest, like a Viking warrior, not letting on any clue to his thoughts. His eyes were shuttered down preventing her from reading his reaction. She thought for sure he'd protest. She had to give him enough reasons to go to Orcas Island, away from the drug dealers who wanted to kill him.

"Lars and Sten said they would take me."

Finn's tight jaw thrust forward, his voice lowering into the deep warning range. "Oh, they did?" Finally, a reaction from the stone face.

Sophie had learned at a very early age to get the Jenkins brothers to do what she wanted by pitting them against each other. The determination to beat the other brother always distracted them from her plan.

Lars sauntered over with the mention of his name. Sten was playing a video game with Tariq, their laughter and grunts could be heard clear across side of the room.

"With the twins as backup, Tariq and I can be on Orcas for dinner with Jordan." Sophie swallowed to suppress the quiver in her voice. Jordan had taken over the role of mother after their mother's death. And after the harrowing day stirring up bad memories, she wanted to be with her older sister.

Finn's eyes flashed to her face. She could never hide anything from him. He was eerily psychic in his ability to discover her deepest desires. But she had learned a few tricks over the years in keeping secrets. She lowered her eyes, away from his scrutiny. Did he see through her plan to protect him?

Lars draped his arm around Sophie's shoulder. "You have a problem with Sten and me helping Soph out, big brother?"

She waited. This was the moment that the boys would start their pissing match. And she had total faith in Finn winning.

Finn's wide grin took her totally by surprise. "Nope. I think it's a great plan."

Suspiciously, Sophie examined Finn's face. "You do?"

Lars squeezed Sophie's shoulder. "It will be great to be on Orcas."

"But..." With her stomach plummeting to her knees, she tried to figure out what had just happened.

"What is it, Soph? I thought you wanted to go to Orcas Island?" Amusement laced Finn's voice.

She had been outplayed. "You and my father already decided that Orcas Island was a safe place for me to be tucked away. Didn't you?"

"Your father is against you leaving, but I know how much you wanted to see Jordan. And Brophy is waiting to meet Tariq."

Finn gave Sophie his most inscrutable look. He was getting rid of her so he could go find the bad guys. But how was he going to be safe if he sent his brothers with her?

"Lars and Sten don't have to come with me. I can have my usual crew. You might need their help." Finn would never admit that the biker gang was after him. Reeves couldn't find anything more about the Honchoes and their connection to Finn's last assignment without hacking into the Navy's server or that at least was what Reeves was claiming. Did Finn instruct Reeves to not share the information with her?

Finn's eyes darkened. It was always shocking since his eyes were a light, iridescent blue, but when he was upset, they turned a dark shade like slate.

"You thought I'd let you go to Orcas Island without me?" Was that hurt in Finn's voice?

"You're going to fly with us to Orcas?" Sophie stepped closer to Finn, wanting...she wasn't sure what she wanted except Finn away from the murdering drug dealers.

"Can't get rid of me that easily. I'm still in charge of your detail until Uncle Harry gets back. And we'll go tomorrow after I have everything in place."

Like the sand under her feet at low tide, Sophie felt the ground shift where she was standing, and pull away from her.

What had just happened? Sophie touched Finn's arm, she didn't want to have the personal conversation with both brothers standing close. "Can we talk, please?"

Finn shook his head, ignoring the sparks flying between them. "We can talk later. I need to get everything organized for tomorrow's flight."

He didn't want to talk. It was an excuse since Finn didn't need to organize the security with three Jenkins brothers, and Jack, Drew, and Reeves all capable of getting them to the airport.

But once she had him alone, that would change. Oh yes, she would make him talk...

Right when she was going to demand Finn and she go back into the conference room and have it out, Danni, her sister's research partner, appeared in the hallway.

"Sophie, are you all right?"

Lars stiffened next to Sophie as the energetic woman rushed down the hallway.

"How did she get into the high security area?" Lars's eyes tracked every step of the gorgeous six-foot woman in her Louboutin suede boots with a matching suede, ultra-short skirt.

"Reeves let her in," Danni threw her long blonde hair over her shoulder like a runway model knowing she raised the testosterone level in the building to the red dangerous zone.

A grin moved across Sophie's face, the first in a while. Danni loved messing with Lars, a confident womanizer like his older brother. And by the way his breathing sped up and his Scandinavian skin flushed, the sexy super soldier was ready to fall at her feet.

"Do you need to frisk me?" Danni purred.

Finn's low rumble of amusement warmed Sophie. She looked up and caught Finn in an intense piercing stare. She couldn't look away from the demanding heat in his eyes.

"Your sister sent me." And the tall woman pulled Sophie into her arms. "She didn't want you to be alone with only these insensitive Neanderthal Jenkins."

Danni leaned back to inspect Sophie's face. "You look like crap, honey." Which made Sophie want to laugh and cry at the same time.

"What did you do to her?" Ballsy Danni pushed forward and got right into Finn's face. "Am I going to have hurt you?"

Sophie bit her lower lip still not clear if she was going to laugh or cry. She hadn't shed a tear, but having Danni close, throwing threats at the Alpha Jenkins brothers, was making it difficult to not fling herself into her friend's strong arms and pour out all of her tightly held feelings. And she might have if Tariq wasn't watching from the video game station.

Finn's face suffused with color and his voice went into the dark, dangerous range. "Why are you here again?"

"OMG. I didn't believe it."

Sophie looked between the two. What was Danni talking about?

Before Sophie could say anything, Lars grabbed Danni's arm turning her to face him. "Back off. They just went through hell and they don't need you busting in to give them crap."

Danni delivered a fierce elbow to Lars's gut who gasped sharply, before he twisted Danni's arm, pulling her hard against his chest. "You'd better be careful who you decide to use your marital arts tricks on."

Undaunted, Danni, flush against Lars's massive chest, batted her eyelashes at him. Lars immediately stepped back and released his hold.

"You're not impressed with my Krav Maga training? But I was just warming up."

Sophie expected sparks to fly off of Lars's face by his red-hot blush. A wide-eyed Lars was a moth flying close to the burning flame when Danni slammed her boot heel into his foot. He shouted, "Damn, woman."

"Next time it won't be your foot that I hurt." Danni flipped her flaxen hair over her shoulder and smirked at Lars before throwing her arm around Sophie. "Let Aunt Danni take care of you away from…"

"That was dirty pool," Lars snarled.

"It's not the only dirty thing I know how to do." Danni batted her eyes again.

Finn slapped his brother on the back. "Come on, bro. Know when to walk away." But Finn stared at Sophie as if the message was for her.

"Soph, where can we get some privacy? Away from…" Danni raised her perfectly arched golden eyebrows.

"Let's go into the conference room." Sophie steered Danni to the room Finn had just exited.

"I was hoping Alex Hardy was going to be here," Danni threw over her shoulder. "Now there's a real man."

Finn and Lars stood shoulder-to-shoulder watching the women. The resemblance between the brothers with their bulging arms crossed over their broad shoulders, feet braced apart with a weary cautious look was comical.

"Soph." Finn stopped Sophie from entering the room.

With her hand on the doorknob, she looked back. "Yes, Finn?"

"We'll be staying upstairs tonight."

Sophie's suspicions alerted. No fight over Orcas or staying at her father's fortress. What was Finn up to? "No problem, as long as we leave for Orcas tomorrow."

Lars huffed. "We are not taking that woman with us to Orcas."

"That woman doesn't want to go." Getting the last word, Danni slammed the door.

CHAPTER THIRTEEN

Gulam threw his head back. Tension building at the base of his spine and the pressure growing in his balls. He was close to exploding.

What the little Irish whores could do with their mouths was worth whatever Asif had paid. Gulam never asked where the porcelain white teens came from. Only that they have skin the color of his mother's alabaster jars, delicate features, not the dark eyes and harsh features of the women of his country and that they be young and innocent. Willing his body to relax into the moment, he opened his eyes enjoying the two sisters working in tandem to bring him pleasure.

The older one knelt next to him, her red hair flaming across his chest like the fire burning in his groin as she pulled him deep into the moist recesses of her mouth. Her younger sister knelt between his legs, talented for her young age, her tongue slowly licking his balls before sucking them deep.

He loved the pale skin of the nubile young women, their hair in hues of orange like the sunsets in Quetta, their breasts bouncing with every pleasurable swipe of their tongues. His blood thickened, heat building underneath his skin—the tantalizing agony before the ecstasy.

Light danced in front of his eyes as time slowed and his entire being focused on release. He pumped into her mouth, wrapping his hands into her hair to force her to take his long mighty cock. The young one pulled hard on his balls and he exploded. He yanked her hair, pleasure riveting him as her delicate throat moved with swallowing his life force.

He fell back on the satin pillow, settling into the sated release.

A knock at the door shattered his replete languor. He would kill Asif for this breach. No one else would dare interrupt him but his cousin.

Keeping his eyes averted, Asif entered the enormous suite. In their youth, he and Asif had shared women but not any longer. Gulam didn't share anything with his subordinates. Besides, Asif was too rough, enjoying eliciting pain.

"This is of the utmost importance." Asif stood frozen at the door.

Gulam flung his hand to dismiss the girls who scurried naked to the adjoining room. Then he reached in the side table for his gun and pointed the barrel straight at Asif's chest. "Five seconds before you're a dead man."

Undaunted, Asif stood tall and waited. "Tariq has been found. We must act immediately if you want him captured."

Gulam should feel relief, but felt nothing. He rolled off the bed, placed the gun back in the drawer, and stood. Asif rushed to the bathroom for a robe. "Where has the little bastard been hiding?"

Donning the warmed robe, he walked to the side bar for the smooth and most expensive Dalmore 62 Scotch. He slowly poured the golden liquid from the heavy decanter into the Glencairn nosing glass. He loved the British rituals for drinking whisky and tea and would not be rushed.

"He's been seen in the Seattle area."

The news was like a fist to his gut. Gulam was scheduled to speak in Seattle. Was this a CIA setup? A way to keep him in the States to bring charges against him without the difficulty of extradition from England.

"How?" He kept his voice even despite his fury. "We had men watching the airport in Kathmandu 24/7."

"I don't know. CJNG's drug couriers had a sighting of him in northern Washington."

"How do we know we aren't being played by our cartel clients to get the reward?"

"The CJNG want exclusive access to our meth to take over the Sinaloa Cartel's turf. They're smart enough to not antagonize us."

"I don't care about the turf wars. Give me the details about this sighting." He paced like a caged animal, trapped in the luxurious presidential suite at 45 Park Lane, his pleasure palace ruined by the news.

Asif stepped back in response to Gulam's rage. "He was accompanied by a blonde woman and two men."

His sister's betrayal delivered another sharp thrust to the gut. "Yasra is with Tariq? In disguise?"

"There is no way of knowing if the blonde is Yasra. The couriers weren't paying attention to the woman—only Tariq."

A foreboding of alarm blast down his spine, slowing his movement. "The CIA helped Tariq and Yasra out of Nepal?"

"CJNG's couriers said they weren't feds but their security was heavy with armed guards."

Why hadn't he killed the little fucker when he had the chance? He worried too much that someone would connect him with the bombing if more of his family members died. It didn't matter now.

"The couriers have them?"

"Tariq and Yasra escaped despite heavy fire from the motorcycle gang on the highway."

"The idiots tried to take them on a public highway? Why not call the police to make sure they got involved?" Gulam spat out his disgust.

Asif shrugged his shoulders. They were both used to the stupidity of their clients. "They were responding to our reward. The couriers are now in FBI/DEA custody. You don't have to worry. They won't talk."

"Not worry?" The slow fury simmering under his skin was ready to detonate. "We know the CIA is looking into me. All I need is one of the bikers or any of my business connections to roll over. Or Tariq to share his memories."

"The CIA isn't involved."

It was hard not to be paranoid when any of his clients wouldn't hesitate to kill him to gain control of his business.

"The CJNG have a high-level informant who has credible intel that it was a Navy SEAL with Tariq and Yasra when the couriers attacked them. The SEAL likely believes the couriers were after him for killing one of CJNG's first lieutenants."

"Why is a SEAL with Tariq and Yasra if they aren't in federal custody?"

"I asked the exact question. He doesn't know why Tariq is with the SEAL or if the woman is Yasra. But it's our first chance of getting Tariq."

"Nothing adds up. I don't like the SEAL. I don't like anything about this operation."

"Our clients can arrange for Tariq's and Yasra's capture by private mercenaries for the reward and a guarantee of expanded meth distribution. But we must decide quickly. Their informant said that Tariq and Yasra are flying out of a private airport today. CJNG is looking into all the private airports right now."

"You don't find this suspicious? You don't think CJNG is setting us up?"

"The CJNG have a lot to lose if we go down. The only reason we have the lead on Tariq and Yasra at the airport is because of CJNG's informant's connection to the SEAL."

"It is one hell of a coincidence."

"It's a win-win for everyone. You get Tariq and Yasra. And they get the SEAL and the meth distribution."

Why didn't it feel like a win? His well-honed sixth sense was recoiling. There were too many unknowns. Still, he couldn't allow Tariq and Yasra to escape. He'd never have this opportunity again, but he hated having limited information when making a critical decision. "Send them a picture of Yasra. They can't kill any of them. Especially a SEAL. It will raise too many questions and I don't want the entire US government looking into the death of a Navy SEAL. My sister and nephew will meet their fate in Pakistan where their disappearance will be less noticed."

He walked toward the window looking out at rain falling on the trees in Hyde Park. "The CJNG will make sure this can't be traced back to me? I want no blowback or the deal is off. And I'll make sure I run them out of the meth business."

"I'll make it very clear what you expect."

Was fate catching up with him for killing his family?

"Rather convenient that I'll be in Seattle to be reunited with my beloved sister and nephew."

CHAPTER FOURTEEN

Leaning against the door, Danni broke into a wide grin. "Taunting the Jenkins boys is becoming one of my favorite activities. Sure beats the hell out of spending all day by my lonesome in the lab." Danni flung her long delicate hands in the air. "OMG. Did you see the way Lars and Finn were staring at us? I wish I had taken my phone out to snap the shot. Hey, boys, can you please hold that 'befuddled, what the hell just happened look?'"

Sophie laughed at the memory of cool and collected Finn not so cool or collected. Danni's outrageous attitude was exactly what Sophie needed after the chase. It helped lighten Sophie's mood to shake Finn's ability to ignore her and their unforgettable kiss—to know that she wasn't the only one flummoxed by what was happening between them—the undeniable heat and desire.

Danni plopped in a chair, crossed her long legs, and swung her booted foot back and forth as she took in every detail of the conference room with its massive-sized screens, computer towers, and an old-school white board. "You have to admit, if you're going to be shot at, the Jenkins boys are mighty fine to have around."

Sophie sat across from her and placed her elbows on Uncle Harry's beat up, wooden table—like the white board, from another era and a startling contrast to the cutting-edge technology in the debriefing room. "Are you admitting that you find Lars attractive?

If I remember right, he was an over-muscled, steroid-enhanced cretin. Not sure if those are the exact words but I think that was the gist."

Danni fingered her amazing white-blonde hair which Sophie always envied—straight and heavy, unlike Sophie's out-of-control curls. "I like messing with him. Men like Lars are used to having women fall all over them. I've found I like beating men at love 'em and leave 'em game. Nothing else. Nothing complicated."

Sophie and Danni shared trust issues with men. Sophie because her father in his grief deserted his daughters after their mother died, and Danni because her fiancé dumped her for a nineteen-year-old model. Not to mention that they both had been kidnapped by Triad rapist-types. Trust issues with a capital T.

"I thought we agreed before you left for Nepal to 'no complications with men.' Just fun and games. But the way Finn was looking at you, as if you were the only woman left on the planet, I'd say that you've broken your promise, and jumped into complicated."

"Hey, we made that promise under duress." Sophie and Danni couldn't endure the flood of worry and sympathy coming from family and friends after the kidnapping. They coped with their "ordeal" by hitting the clubs.

"You call dancing all night duress?"

"And a few tequila shots."

"Girls gotta have fun. Besides it isn't every day that a girl gets kidnapped." Danni rolled her golden hazel eyes. "Did Nepal help the nightmares and the flashbacks?"

"Some. It was helpful to be away from everything and everyone. Not having anything familiar. Everything new and exciting."

"Are we talking about sex with Alex Hardy? Give your bestie some details. Is he as good as Tiffany Lawson revealed to *US* magazine?"

"You read the tabloids?" Danni was an MIT geneticist and the reason why she, along with Jordan were kidnapped—to help in the genetic research the criminals wanted to sell on the dark web.

"You can only read so many scientific journals. And there is no fashion in research journals. And don't think I didn't notice that you deflected about sex and Alex Hardy."

"I wasn't deflecting."

"Sure, and I'm a virgin."

Sophie burst into fits of laughter, letting go of her tension and suppressed feelings. Danni, like Sophie, didn't believe in holding back. In her rebellious days Sophie mastered outrageous for shock benefit. And having a rich and famous daddy helped her shock MO to become regular newsfeed. But Sophie left it behind—like her bad boyfriends and partying.

Sophie shifted in the wooden chair. "Nothing happened."

"You think I'm going to sell your secrets to the tabloids to pay off my student loans?"

"You're kidding? Right? Nothing happened between Alex and me. Girl Scout's honor."

Danni snorted. "You were a Scout?"

"You need to ask?" They hooted with laughter. "Nothing happened between Alex and me. We did the fundraiser together and then we hiked in Nepal."

"Are you kidding? You were alone in a tent on a mountain top with *People* magazine's sexiest man and didn't explore every racy cranny and crevice of that man's body?"

"Your mountain metaphors suck." Sophie smirked. "We were in separate tents. And he could only stay for one night."

"Are you mentioning sucking for a reason?"

"You really need to get out of the lab more."

"Nice try." Danni tapped her long, lean finger on the table. Although her hands were covered in rings, her fingernails were short without polish—a sign of her inner scientist nerd which Danni tried hard to hide.

"I know it worried me...but honestly..." Sophie wasn't sure how to explain her feelings. "I know it's going to sound crazy."

"You're afraid you're going to sound crazy to me? Do you remember what I did after Jax dumped me?"

Sophie reached across the scarred table and patted Danni's

hand. "But that was a normal reaction to a shocking betrayal."

"Trying to run him down in a crosswalk?"

"You swerved at the last minute." They shared a look before they snickered again. Danni was better medicine than any therapist her father wanted her to see. Again.

"Back to your crazy." Danni raised those perfect eyebrows.

"All right, all right. It felt like it was the same bullshit game. 'You're hot. I'm hot. The sex between us is going to be exceptional.'" Until she said the words aloud, Sophie hadn't realized the reason she hadn't rushed into anything with Alex Hardy. She wanted more than a brief fling. Despite his altruistic interest in the plight of refugees, he was exactly like all her past relationships. And like all her past relationship, the relationship with Alex would have played out the same way with amicable, "we're cool" breakup after the lust burnt out.

Danni crossed and uncrossed her legs. "Hot damn. That's exactly what I want. The 'you're hot and I'm hot and let's have exceptional sex.' I'll be happy to get bored with that routine."

"Alex is coming to Seattle. I can introduce you."

Danni flashed the most innocent, sweet smile which spelled double trouble. "Cool. And I don't mind being seconds with Alex Hardy." She tried to cover up the wistfulness in her voice. But Sophie heard the hurt loud and painfully clear. Sophie was all too familiar with pretending that all was cool when it wasn't—like being second in line for your fiancé.

"I'd like to hit Jax in a crosswalk."

Danni chuckled in her deep sexy voice. "Where did that come from?"

"The man was an idiot to let you go."

"Thanks, sweetie. But I'm over Jax and his child girlfriend."

Yeah, Sophie got it. Denial was a fine way of coping. She was wisecracking with Danni to downplay that bikers tried to kill Finn or how about the biggest kahuna of self-deception that Finn's kiss meant nothing. She never allowed herself to think of Finn in any way but as a family friend since she was eighteen-years-old when she shed her adolescent crush.

"Enough of Jax. Did Finn finally man up to his feelings? We've all been waiting."

Sophie jerked stiff in her chair. "What?"

"We've all been waiting for him to declare himself."

"Back up. Who is everyone and why has no one mentioned this little piece of info before?"

"Jordan and me."

"That's everyone?"

"And Reeves, and most likely Finn's brothers and Uncle Harry, but I haven't asked the brothers or Uncle Harry."

"This is a joke." Her body heated in seconds like she had been zapped in a microwave on high. Her world tilted off its axis. There was only so much a girl could take on a given day. And today was climbing the charts.

"Jordan said we had to wait for Finn. That I wasn't to say a word since I'm a bit 'sour' on men and that might influence what I said to you about Finn."

"This is some elaborate bet you have with Reeves?"

Danni blinked—her eyes glassy for a brief moment. "You think I'd mess with you about something important? It took all my self-control not to tell you before you left for Nepal. You deserve a man who loves you—someone who's going to stick. Not some media freak musician or a lothario SEAL."

Sophie's mind was spinning like a merry-go-round on speed. Blurred images of Finn flashed by: his gentleness, his caring concern, his tender touches after the kidnapping. She blinked her eyes and looked around the room to make sure she wasn't hallucinating or beamed to another planet. Finn was being more than a friend after the kidnapping? She was an observant person, a caring person who paid attention to how people were feeling, especially people she loved. Her mind halted to a dead stop. People she loved.

"What's going through that brain of yours?" Danni's cat-like eyes were locked on hers.

"So, you don't approve of either Alex or Finn?" *Deflect and deny* was Sophie's often-used mantra.

"Alex for fun. But Finn—the jury is still out about his reputation."

"His reputation? Is that the kettle calling the pot? You know what I mean...my exploits are viral."

"But you were acting out of hurt. What's his excuse—proving he's the man with a big dick?"

How could a discussion of Finn and his...make her entire body flood with hot chills? She shifted in the chair away from Danni's laser stare. She didn't want to think of Finn's... *Deny, deny.*

"OMG. You already hooked up with Finn."

"No! So, you can get the gleam out of your eyes." No way was she going to dish on that spellbinding kiss now. Not before she talked to Finn. This was too private even to share with Danni.

"Why wouldn't Jordan tell me? We share everything."

"She didn't want to interfere because she loves you both."

That did sound like her sister—always doing the right thing. "Finn isn't exactly shy with women." Refusing to believe that serial player Finn was pining after her, Sophie shook her head adamantly. "I know Finn. He has no trouble going after a woman he wants."

"Obviously, not Sophie Dean. You're not one of his hoochies. You're hot, rich, famous...should I go on? Finn is a regular dude whose uncle works for your father."

"Being a Navy SEAL is being a regular dude?"

"You know what I mean. He doesn't see himself as marriage material for the tech billionaire's daughter."

Sophie snorted. "Now I know this is a joke—Finn and I married?"

Danni raised her hands in the air in surrender. "I got a bit carried away. My theory is that he doesn't think he's good enough which helps my opinion of a Jenkins. But it's only a theory. Who knows? He might have wives scattered all over the world. So, I'm still on the fence. But Jordan is definitely on Team Finn but said she won't give an opinion since she doesn't want to influence you. I have no such compunction. The Jenkins brothers get what they deserve for their blatant sexism."

Sophie stared at Danni, trying to process everything. "This is the way you comfort me after getting shot at?"

"I wanted to take your mind off the shooting. Did it work?"

Sophie tried hard not to grin back at Danni. "It did."

But secretly her heart was hammering like the bass guitar of Full Metal Jacket. The overpowering sound was nothing close to the overpowering emotions hurtling through her brain and body.

CHAPTER FIFTEEN

"Keep it together, man." Finn punched the elevator button. His pep talk sounded more like the twins than his totally self-confident self. He took a slow, deep breath trying to block out the unfamiliar and unwanted sensation hurling in his gut—fear.

For a warrior who prided himself on being fearless, the possibility of losing Sophie today brought back a memory that he had locked away and buried—two Marines in their dress uniforms standing at the Jenkins's front door with their rigid postures and their somber expressions. The wounds will heal but the scars will never fade.

Focus. Compartmentalize those feelings of a frightened fourteen-year-old. Forget the sounds of his calm mother falling to her knees and screaming in agony, the twins and Cooper crying, the sound of Nick's fist smashing through the wall.

He took a deep breath. Focus only on today's mission—check on Sophie and Tariq and then get the hell away. He felt like an idiot that he had been avoiding this confrontation, afraid of how he might react.

Nodding to Tom, a retired Seattle police officer who stood guard at the door, Finn swiped the electronic key to the safe apartment above HQ. It was more of a penthouse than an apartment since nothing in the Deans' world was standard issue.

No one was in the massive, modern, glass and steel living room, decorated with art that was worth more than his annual salary. It was unlike any utilitarian safe house in the Spec-Ops sphere he'd ever inhabited. The deep brown leather couch wasn't wide enough for him to fully stretch out but he planned to sleep on it anyway. Anyone who came through the door would have to go through him to get to Sophie. He was taking no chances after today's "event."

The silence piqued Finn's caution. At seven p.m., he expected Sophie and Tariq to be hanging out in the living room. Had Sophie already gone to sleep? Disappointment flooded Finn. He spent the afternoon and evening with the visceral memory burning through him of Sophie's heavy breasts molded to his chest and the way her tongue danced with his.

Slowly moving across the living room, on alert, he heard the murmur of voices from the second bedroom. He hesitated at the door, then slowly pushed it open. Sophie was snuggled against Tariq with her arm around his shoulder, reading *Harry Potter* aloud in Punjabi from her device. Tariq's eyes were barely open and his head lolled against Sophie's shoulder.

Seeing Sophie, spoiled rich girl on the covers of tabloids, tucked into bed with a Pakistani orphan and all his disciplined, logical compartmentalizing—all his emotions held tight in a little box—blew like C-4 into smithereens. This was the sweet, sensitive girl who followed him around after his father's death, who sensed the pain he kept bottled up. The woman he needed more than air itself.

She nodded to Finn before slipping her arm from behind Tariq, kissing him gently on the top of his dark head. She slipped out of bed, tucking the comforter up to Tariq's neck.

And then Finn's heart did a dive, a deep dive into the swirling arctic waters, where the frigid air knocked your breath out of your lungs.

Sophie wore oversized, red flannel pajamas with reindeers on them. The baggy pajamas couldn't hide the curvy, sexy body. This wasn't the Sophie the world knew in her designer clothes from Paris and Tokyo but the tender woman few were privileged to get glimpses of.

"Reindeers?" Finn's normally steady slow heart rate was blowing in the three-digit range, but he could keep his cool, Jenkins bad-ass facade.

Sophie put her finger to her lips to hush him and all he could think of was sucking on the finger.

"It's barely October." Finn leveled his voice. To stand still and watch Sophie bend over to turn off the light was harder than any challenge the Navy threw at him.

He held the door for Sophie to pass by and was overwhelmed by the scent of citrus and the sultry smell of Sophie. Watching her saunter into the large living room/dining area, took all of his control. He could feel his pulse pounding in his ears and all his blood flow heading south.

"Did you have dinner?" How could Sophie sound so normal when he was about to blow?

"What?"

"You've been downstairs for hours."

Since Sophie and Danni emerged from the incident room, she was back to her confident, in-your-face self. The fear haunting her eyes had vanished. He wasn't sure what Danni and she had shared, but the spunky sex goddess was back. And why did that make him excited and nervous?

"Yeah, Lars got Mexican takeout. What did you and the kid eat? Fresh salmon and risotto?"

He and Sophie shared a conspiratorial grin. Richard Dean had a full-time staff that maintained fresh food at all the properties he owned including the safe apartment.

"No, we ate Mexican too. I didn't feel like cooking tonight."

"Like you ever feel like cooking."

Teasing Sophie was helping Finn feel a little steadier on his feet. He already knew everything Sophie and Tariq had done over the last few hours. Reeves and Sten gave him regular updates. Surprisingly, no one gave him shit about his interest in Sophie. It was pathetic that he hadn't manned up and was relying on his brothers' and Reeves's reports to avoid interacting with Sophie.

"Same as you. Sten brought it. Tariq has never eaten Mexican food. He loved the nachos."

"Don't know any boy or man who doesn't love nachos." Finn grimaced at the inane conversation.

Sophie sat on the leather couch tucking her feet beneath her. Dean's designer, cold angles, metals, and leather was a striking contrast to Sophie's soft blonde curls dangling around her shoulders and her round, shining face and curvaceous body. Everything about her was comfortingly familiar, yet edgy and exciting.

"Any news about the Honchoes?"

Not exactly what he was thinking of, but like always, Sophie wasn't going to let him avoid the topic. "I spoke with a DEA agent I know from California. He really didn't have any reason why they would come after us." Finn moved away from the couch, away from the biggest temptation.

"Really, Finn?" Sophie jumped up, moving into his space, and poked her puny finger into his chest. "You're going to try to bullshit me?"

Finn stood frozen, his hands clenched at his side, suppressing the impulse to grab her, aware of her siren scent, her intake of breath and the view of her soft luminescent skin where the "v" to her pajamas opened.

Sophie stopped her prodding, her mouth hung wide open. He must not be doing a great job of hiding his white-hot drive to claim, to own this one tiny woman.

"Why did you kiss me?"

Finn stepped back a step with Sophie following. It was always like this between them—Sophie pushing, never letting him slide. After the loss of his close SEAL team member, he returned home angry and bitter over another senseless loss. Sophie sensing his pain, wouldn't allow him to wallow in his misery, drawing him out with her tender, probing concern. This confirmed everything he had been running from for years. Sophie was the only woman for him. Forced him to feel. Made him human.

"I was worried after what went down in Hong Kong that today might have triggered memories."

"That was a kiss of concern?" Her lips pursed in a knowing half smile—a modern, curly-headed Mona Lisa.

Finn clenched his hands into fists and ground his teeth trying to not grab Sophie and kiss the amusement out of her voice. To finally show her exactly and explicitly how he felt about her.

Sophie circled her finger on his chest, not prodding but playing—playing with burning hell fire. "Sounds about right. Finn Jenkins kissing damsels in distress."

He grabbed her finger, pressing her hand against his heart. He had a choice to lie, but he was tired of running, hiding, pretending. With CJNG coming after him, today might be his only chance. "No, Soph. Only you. It's always been only you."

"Since when, Finn?" Sophie brushed the curls away from her eyes and looked deep into his, not letting him dodge the truth. Sparks of electric sexual tension ricocheted between them. "This isn't some exaggerated response to your guilt over Hong Kong?"

Since when? If he told her the truth would she run? He rubbed his thumb along her silky soft hand. "I'm never going to forget what those days felt like when you were missing. And yes, I'll always blame myself for leaving you and Uncle Harry."

Sophie moved closer leaving a mere inch between them, ramping up the heated tension. Now he was breathing like a newbie SEAL dragging a log out of the Pacific Ocean.

"We really have to work on your exaggerated sense of responsibility for everyone in the world."

Finn slid his hands along Sophie's arms, ignoring the pain of his erection pressing against his jeans zipper. His voice roughening with need. "You can work on me in any way you want, Soph."

"That sounded like one of your practiced lines."

Finn watched the way Sophie's breath hitched and the exposed skin in the silly pajamas turn pink. As if the oxygen had been sucked out of the room, he couldn't get a breath. "God. No. Just wishful thinking."

"This is all still a shock for me. First the kiss and then Danni telling me about your feelings."

Hell, Finn felt the heat climbing the back of his neck as his balls clenched in need. "That woman. What does she know?"

"Don't change the subject, Finn Jenkins." Sophie moved against him, losing that last inch, taking him to boiling point with his erection swelling to no return.

"It's complicated." His breath came in harsh bursts with Sophie's curves pressed to him. "Us—we're complicated."

Sophie rubbed those outstanding breasts against him, and there was no way Finn could hide his raging hard-on pressing against her stomach, or the way his body was clenched and ready.

"Doesn't feel complicated. Feels straightforward to me." And there was the sexy teasing making him want to drag her to the floor and show her how straightforward he could be. His self-control was evaporating.

He stepped back and ran his hand through his hair. "Sophie, this isn't the time. You got shot at today and need comfort." Like after Hong Kong, he wanted to be the man who comforted and protected her, not the one who took advantage like all the assholes before him. "But hell, it never feels like it's been the right time for us."

Sophie stood on her tiptoes and wrapped her arms around his neck. "I'm not going to pretend that today wasn't difficult, but I realized in the moment of danger that I wasn't afraid. And I don't mean because you can shoot and outrun and all the bad-ass stuff you do but because I trust you. I'll always trust you. As long as you're near, my world is safe and complete."

"Just trust, Sophie?" He dragged his thumb along her pale neck before he tucked a curl behind her ear. "Because I want more than trust."

"I want more too." Sophie pressed against him, grinding her heat into him. "I resigned myself to being friends to never allow myself to hope for more."

Finn's body tightened in rampaging need, his brain went into the danger zone. Sophie making the moves on him was the moment he had been waiting for it seemed his whole life. Despite the need to drive himself into her wet moist heat, this moment was more than a need to get off. This was Sophie. "What about Alex Hardy?"

Sophie unbuttoned the top button of her pjs. "Who?"

Finn froze as the open buttons revealed more perfect pale skin. "Sophie, what is going on here?"

"With your experience, I assumed you'd figure that out by now. I want you, Finn Jenkins. I've wanted you since... I don't know from what age. I thought it was a teenage crush when you came back from BUD/S all sexy and confident. I tucked it away never believing we'd ever be more than friends when you treated me like a kid sister." She touched his cheek, skimming her fingers along his jaw, burning a path of need. "I want everything with you."

"After Hong Kong, I tried to show you how much I cared but you went off to Nepal with Alex Hardy."

Sophie exhaled loudly in exasperation exposing more skin, giving him a glimpse of her large pink nipples. And all Finn wanted was to latch his mouth and suck until Sophie begged him, begged him to do what he had been waiting for his entire life.

"I thought you were being overprotective because you felt guilty. It wasn't until today that I started to reconsider..."

Self-deprecation rushed through Finn despite his raging body focused on one thing—thrusting into Sophie over and over. He couldn't believe he was able to speak. "Well, that's not exactly a compliment to my skills if you needed Danni." His finger, of its own will, was tracing the "v" on Sophie's pjs, needing to touch her.

Sophie tugged on her bottom lip. "I've been lying to myself all this time about the trip to Orcas Island, pretending it was only for Tariq. When in fact, I wanted an excuse to be with you—to relive the memories and make new ones to get me through the lonely times ahead without you."

Unable to squeeze out a single word, afraid he was in a dream, Finn froze.

"What's wrong?" Sophie rotated her hips knowing damn well what she was doing to him. "Did your stab wound affect you and your...?"

Finn laughed out loud at Sophie's outrageous question. "Everything is in working order as you can feel." He grabbed Sophie's wandering hands between his and lifted her into his arms. "Sophie Dean, we are about to get complicated."

"You promise?"

CHAPTER SIXTEEN

Sophie leaned against Finn's rock-hard chest as he carried her to her room. Not sure if this was real or a dream, she stared at his chiseled jaw, his glimmering eyes dark with arousal, tension telegraphing from his body.

Finn Jenkins, childhood friend, and the star of every one of her adolescent fantasies, wanted her.

He looked down at her, catching her staring. "What is it, Soph? Changing your mind?" His jaw locked and Sophie knew how much it took him to utter those words by the way his teeth ground back and forth.

"Really, you need to ask?" She ran her fingers throughs his scruffy beard. "I'm trying to believe this is real. That this isn't one of my teenage daydreams when Finn Jenkins carries me off. Or that this is some joke you and your brothers have cooked up."

Finn's hard chest radiated heat, warming Sophie through her pajamas. She snuggled closer as they entered the spacious black and gray master bedroom with slick silver mirrors. The same cold, male motif the designer had done for all her father's properties. Nothing to warm her except hot, sexy Finn.

He lowered her slowly down his body. "Does this feel like a joke?" His chuckle vibrated against her.

He lifted her chin with his calloused thumb. "Soph, are you sure this is what you want? You're not just trying to make me feel better?"

"Do you promise to make me feel better too?"

He pushed a curl behind her ear, his finger lingering on the sensitive spot behind her ear. "I plan to make you a helluva lot better."

"Then I say it's a win-win." Sophie was trying to keep up her cool banter, not letting Finn see how deeply she was affected by Finn's hunger for her, Sophie Dean, the young girl who followed and bugged him their entire time growing up together.

When she realized that Finn Jenkins had no interest in her except as friends, she moved on. Her mind might be having trouble with the idea of Finn as her lover, but her body was totally onboard by the feel of his hot, demanding body.

Finn unbuttoned her ridiculous pajamas; she had worn them to amuse Tariq and they weren't seductive drive-men-crazy clothes. His rough fingers rubbed against her over-sensitized skin.

"You are so sexy in these pajamas. Better than my imagination could conjure when I'm undressing you in my mind."

Sophie grabbed Finn's hand from the buttons. "Finn, tell me one fantasy you've had about me when I'm not in reindeer pajamas."

Color spotted Finn's cheeks. And he took a sharp inhale. "You're trying to torture me?"

Sophie lifted his hand to her mouth and teased each finger with her tongue before she lifted his index finger into her mouth and sucked. Staring into Finn's darkening eyes, she purred, "I thought we could act out one of those fantasies."

Finn's chest heaved while his eyes remained on her mouth. Sophie had played seducing Finn in her head so many times—the inventive ways that she would bring the competent, confident, sexy SEAL to beg.

"Later, later we can do anything you want, but right now I want to taste you and hear you scream my name. I've wanted only my name on your lips. You needy, wanting only me."

Sophie's knees buckled. Hell, she was already lost, lost in his pale eyes, lost in his explicit words. Already willing to beg him.

Finn's hands were shaking as he finished unbuttoning her top.

He slipped it partially off before running his tongue along the sensitive spot between her neck and shoulder sending shivers along the wet path.

His hot hands held her arms in place while he continued the sensual torture before he tore her top off and then stared at her bare breasts. The cool air lifted and puckered her nipples.

"How can reality be so much better? Your nipples are big and perfect for my mouth." Finn flicked his thumbs over her nipples, shooting a straight shot downward. Heat, need, and moisture blossomed between her legs before he took one nipple into his mouth. She had to grab his arm to steady herself from the sensory overload.

He bent and pulled her pajama bottoms down as she stepped out. He paused on his knees for a view of her exposed flesh. "Christ, Soph," he panted. "The sight of you is mind-blowing."

His finger trailed between the folds, triggering a need to spread her legs further apart. He pushed her back until her knees hit the back of the bed and then down so she was sprawled over the cover.

"Spread your legs, honey. I want to see all of you. I've waited so long."

Losing all modesty by the fierce demand in Finn's voice, Sophie wantonly threw herself back exposing herself as she pulled her knees to her chest.

"You're killing me, Soph." Leaning over her, he tweaked her clit between his thumb and forefinger sending her almost off the bed. And then his mouth and tongue were pressed against her as he drove her crazy, teasing the twitching bundle of nerves.

She grabbed his head, her fingers digging into his scalp as she pushed him against her mound. "Finn," she pleaded.

Finn parted her folds with his fingers as his tongue moved faster taking her higher. Her back arched inching closer to the peak. He pushed two fingers into her while his mouth tugged, and Sophie clamped her legs around his head. Her entire body shook with the force of her orgasm, vibrant colors twirling before her eyes as she sunk into happy oblivion.

Breathless, she threw herself to the center of the bed.

Finn stood and tugged his shirt over his head at the same time unbuckling his belt. He quickly pulled his pants and boxers down.

"The rumors were true." Sophie giggled at her first sight of Finn and his impressive anatomy.

And despite her mindless, sated state, she pushed up on her elbows to not miss the impressive Finn Jenkins undressing. A red, puckered scar crossed his abdomen where he had been stabbed. She came to her knees and leaned forward to touch the wound. "Are you sure you're up for this, Finn? Does it hurt?"

Finn was sheathing his hard length into a condom he had dug out of his pocket. His usually light eyes were the color of the turbulent Lake Washington. "It will only hurt if I'm not inside you right now."

"I can help you without putting any strain on your scar." She ran her finger along his length, enjoying the response.

"Not that I don't appreciate your offer. I plan to take you up on it later since one of my favorite fantasies is you on your knees in the shower."

Her nipples tightened and her body hummed by the visual he created.

"Soph, I've waited too many years longing for you. But if you've changed your mind. I understand."

And there was the boy that Sophie had loved her whole life. Always protecting others before himself.

Didn't he understand how long she had been waiting for Finn Jenkins, naked and needing her?

"There is no going back, Soph. This will change everything. Because once you're mine, I'm never letting you go."

She fell back on the bed and opened her arms. "And I'm never letting you go. You belong to me, Finn Jenkins."

"It's all I've ever wanted—to belong to you, Sophie Dean." He covered her with his body, the rough hair on his chest abrading her sensitive skin and nipples. She wrapped her legs around him, bringing her heat next to him, then arched her hips to bring him even closer.

"Honey, I can't wait." He pushed in with one hard, slick plunge. His big hands lifted her hips higher for a deeper penetration. His features hardened in concentration and sweat beaded on his forehead.

She could do nothing but feel, the heat coming in strong waves as he took her with slow, delicious drives. She moaned his name as the pleasure mounted.

He thrust into her again and again as he bit lightly on her hard nipples.

A rush of pleasure surged so high and fast that she couldn't breathe.

"Sophie, look at me."

She stopped her thrashing and opened her eyes to Finn's intense stare. "You're mine, Sophie." He made a growling, triumphant sound as he lifted one of her legs over her shoulder to open her further. "Mine. Only mine."

His thrusts took her straight into mindless pleasure. He stayed with her riding every drawn-out spasm until she was limp, boneless, blown over the edge of sanity.

He buried his face against her neck, letting out a strangled moan as his plunges grew harder. She felt his stomach muscles clench as the raw power of the passion of his release filled her. His erratic breathing slowed and he collapsed on top of her.

His heat and weight were a salve to her soul. She didn't know how much she needed his strength and comfort until this moment.

He pulled back to look at her. "Pretty quiet? What is going through that brain of yours, Soph?"

She held his beautiful face between her hands at a loss for words. It would be so cliché to say she never knew it could be like this.

Finn tenderly brushed his lips over hers. "It's the same for me, Soph." And he rolled off of her, taking her with him pulling her next to him.

Sophie snuggled closer against Finn's sculpted chest, missing his heat.

He smoothed her hair which was one ratty mess by now. She circled his nipple with her fingertip, liking the sudden intake of his breath.

"Finn, why did you wait?"

He let out a loud sigh. "Because I'm not the best choice for you. If I weren't a selfish bastard, I'd never have touched you. But after today, I decided I may never get the chance to be with you."

"Isn't it up to me to decide who is a bad choice?" Sophie tweaked his nipple hard. "You've always thought you knew what was best for me."

"Ow. That hurt, woman. And after some of your choices…"

"Finn Jenkins. Of all the nerve to compare my boyfriends… when your choices weren't any better. Should I remind you about Jeannine Newbill or Rosemary Fry?"

Finn moaned dramatically. "Okay, all right. But Soph. You deserve…"

"What do I deserve? A rich businessman like my father? A rock star who's more interested in having our pictures taken together? Is that what I deserve?"

He placed his larger hand over hers to stop her from pinching him again. "You deserve a man who will love and protect you."

"Damn straight, Finn Jenkins." She propped herself on to one elbow to look into his eyes. "And will you be that man?"

"You know I will as long as you want me."

"I'll never not want you, Finn."

"Sophie, you do know that SEALs don't make good partners. Our jobs are demanding and risky."

"Is this your way of convincing me? I have to say you need to work on your approach. Being a SEAL is who you are. Protecting the people and country you love is part of your makeup. It's in your Jenkins DNA. Or is this something to do with today's shootout and your belief they're coming after you?"

"Where did you come up with that idea?"

Sophie grabbed his chin and turned his head toward her. "Finn Jenkins, I understand your work is classified, but don't shut me out with your medieval ideas that you're protecting me."

"It's my job to protect you."

Sophie chewed on her lower lip and counted backwards from ten in Farsi. "Not communicating, not sharing your worries, is not the same as protecting me."

"That was my point about not telling you how I felt about you. My work is not something I can share with you."

"But you can share if you're worried or if something was difficult, right?"

"Yes." Finn's eyes were narrowed as if he was expecting some sort of trap.

"All I ask, Finn, is that you share your feelings with me."

"Okay." Finn nudged his hard erection against her thigh. "You know how I'm feeling, Soph?"

"Now that wasn't too 'hard' to share, was it?" Sophie punched him in the arm.

Finn's breathing got harsh. "Very funny pun. You want to play, little girl?"

Sophie crawled on top of his chest, rubbing her heat against his chest. "You remember when we played cowboys as kids?"

Finn's fingers gripped her hips.

"Ready to be ridden, cowboy?"

CHAPTER SEVENTEEN

Every protective cell in Finn's body was on full alert as Nick drove slowly through the private gate to Richard Dean's hangar. There was no going back after last night after finally having Sophie. She was now his. His to love. His to protect. And he wouldn't relax until Sophie and Tariq were tucked in the "castle," the code name for Dean's mansion on Orcas Island. No one would ever get close to her again on his watch. No one messed with his woman and got to live.

Lars and Sten had arrived ahead of them to clear the area. Dean's hangar housed his four jets and two helicopters armed with the latest in security cameras monitored 24/7. The twins waited in their SUV angled in front of the plane. Jack and Drew followed.

Adrenaline pulsed, sharpening his awareness, and pumping his muscles in readiness. One of the riskiest moments in a security detail was the transfer of the package from the car to the plane, exposing everyone as they climbed the stairs.

He reassured himself that the Honchoes were in custody and even if they made contact with CJNG, the drug cartel had no way of knowing Finn's plans.

"Finn, did you hear? Tariq wants to know if all Americans own their own jets." Sophie leaned forward from the back seat, bringing a whiff of the sunny scent of her citrus shampoo. Finn didn't turn to get closer and inhale the scent of Sophie.

Both he and Sophie were acting as if nothing had occurred

between them, as if last night hadn't rocketed them both into a new stratosphere. It might fool Tariq but he doubted it fooled his brothers, trained observers. And the way Sophie blushed when she came downstairs was enough for Finn to blow their agreement to keep their relationship on the down low and to kiss her senseless.

He focused on scanning the area for armed drug dealers. And pretending that the images of Sophie riding him, Sophie on her knees in the shower weren't burned into his brain.

"No, I missed it." Sophie and Tariq chattered away on the drive over as if nothing out of the ordinary happened this morning. In contrast, Finn was hyper-vigilant, keenly aware of every car at every intersection on the thirty-minute route from Queen Anne.

"Finn, do you think Reeves can visit me on Orcas Island?" Tariq asked. "He promised me he would come. Will my new uncle allow him?"

"I'm sure Mr. Brophy will. I can't think of a reason he wouldn't," Sophie reassured.

Surrounded by threats, Finn hadn't considered how difficult the transition to Orcas Island would be for Tariq, especially being separated from Sophie. Finn could sympathize how cold it felt to be away from Sophie.

Nick swerved into the hangar to position Sophie directly across from the stairwell. Finn scanned the entire area including the next hangar which housed the helo tour and flight school with several helicopters parked in front. The sprawling complex of Boeing Field was both a private and commercial airfield. Flight school businesses, charter flights, and other private airplanes shared the airstrip.

Today the team was miked. Finn was treating it as a high-risk mission and his brothers and Uncle Harry were in agreement of the extreme level of danger if CJNG was involved. "Lars, did you sweep both Dean's and the helo school's hangar?"

"Yes, boss. The helo business is locked up dark. Looks like they're not running flights today."

The little hairs on Finn's neck rose though he saw nothing alarming. In his SEAL world this kind of extraction was the bread and butter of missions. But having the woman he loved as the package had Finn wired. He sucked in and blew out a breath. "Showtime."

"We got this covered, bro." Nick turned off the ignition. Thank God he had his brothers around him, balancing out his ramped-up adrenaline and overload of emotions. And thank God for Uncle Sam's training in compartmentalizing since Sophie's nearness was playing havoc with his cool.

Jack and Drew parked their vehicle facing outward for a fast exit. The team was in sync which should have been reassuring yet, it didn't stop the same free-falling sensation in Finn's gut he got when leaping from thirty thousand feet into the black night.

His brothers circled the plane, taking their positions. Lars, his M4 carbine at his side, took the back of the plane while Sten covered the front. Finn hadn't wanted to alarm Sophie and Tariq but the team was heavily packing side arms and assault rifles.

The team was treating today as if they were bringing a high target extraction out of a hostile country instead of a trip to Orcas Island. With the image of Hong Kong and the Honchoes fixed into every memory cell, Finn wasn't taking any risks. This wasn't exactly how either he or Sophie imagined their trip.

Nick gave Finn a nod before exiting the front doors. Finn climbed out and opened Sophie's door while Nick helped Tariq scramble out of the high SUV. Finn ignored his pounding heartbeat and the heat rushing into his body with every twist Sophie had to make to climb out of the SUV. He shut down the image of Sophie rocking against him when he was buried deep from behind. He scanned the area one last time before holding out his hand for her.

Sophie squeezed his hand, her voice silky like last night's sheets. "Thank you." And then she gave him her mega-watt sexy smile, the one that had men of every age willing to crawl over broken glass to be the recipient. "Last night was better than any fantasy I've had about you."

Finn was left staring as Sophie strutted to the stairwell. Leave it up to Sophie to distract him when he needed to bring his "A" game today. Finn jolted at the sound of Tariq cracking up from something Nick had said to him as the two moved together toward the stairwell.

Finn's sixth sense was hopping around like Mexican jumping beans. "Get in the plane, Sophie." His voice came out sharper than he intended and had Nick shooting him a *what-the-hell-is-wrong-with-you* look.

Sophie stopped at the first step, her foot in the air, and turned back to glare at him. "Really?"

He turned abruptly to the sound of the helo business's newest H130, the logo of Heroic Heli School blazing on its body, arriving. He watched as did his brothers. The helo didn't land in front of their hangar, but instead landed directly in front of Dean's hangar, blocking their exit, the whirling of blades deafening and the resulting wind tunnel sucking air out of the space.

"What the hell?" Nick pulled out his Glock.

Four armed men in full battle gear jumped from the helo. Well-orchestrated and well-trained, the men moved across the five hundred feet in seconds toward Sophie. Finn ran the five feet to Sophie when shots pinged off Sten and Lar's SUV. The bastards were using silencers to not alert anyone to the full assault.

Nick pushed Tariq to the ground in front of the car before he rushed forward to cover Sophie and Finn who were wide open.

An enraged Finn grabbed Sophie who stood frozen by the stairwell. A shot ricocheted off Dean's plane before Finn could pull Sophie to the ground. Knocked out of his usual battle zone of no emotion, Finn surged with the need to tear the men apart one by one.

Suddenly smoke filled the space making it impossible to see. Tasting and smelling the phosphoric acid, Finn lurched forward to lift Sophie off her feet—they had thrown smoke grenades into the hangar. And by the diminishing visibility, they threw multiple military-grade smoke grenades.

He ran into the haze where the SUV was parked. He searched for the door and threw Sophie into the back. "Get down. Lock the door and do not get out, no matter what."

He slammed the door when he heard the sound of footsteps coming from the rear of the SUV—more than one pair moving toward them. He pulled his SIG out of the back of his jeans. He'd nail these bastards if they thought they could take him or Sophie.

Finn shoved Nick, whom he could feel next to him, and yelled at him, "Get Sophie and Tariq out of here. I'll cover you while you get Tariq."

Nick's pissed-off voice came through the smog while he shoved the car keys in Finn's hand. "Stupid fucker. Get in the fricking SUV and get out of here."

Then the other brothers shouted through their mics, first Lars, then Sten. "Finn, get the hell out of here," Lars shot.

"We can handle these suckers once we can see them," Sten added.

Finn felt the rush of air when Nick scurried toward Lars's voice. "They're headed my way."

Before moving to get Tariq, Finn listened for approaching footsteps from his rear. With his gun pointed into the lifting fog, he moved to the front of the SUV to grab Tariq who must be scared crazy. "Tariq, I'm coming for you, little man." Finn ran his left hand, his gun-free hand, along the SUV to guide him to the front of the oversized vehicle.

Finn heard the haste of multiple scurrying feet toward the outside of the hangar at the same time as the roaring sound of the helo getting reading to take off. They were leaving? He looked back at the SUV. Sophie would have screamed if they'd somehow gotten to her.

Finn rushed toward the front of the hangar away from the smoke. A limp Tariq was hanging from one of the men's arms who was boarding the helo. Two men aimed AR15s at Finn as if daring him to run into the gunfire. Daring him to commit suicide.

CHAPTER EIGHTEEN

Sophie lay on the floor of the SUV. Her breathing was staccato, her heart furiously beating against her chest in painful strikes. Armed men jumped from a helicopter and pointed their guns directly at her and Finn. Her heart lurched in an agonizing thud with flashbacks of armed men in the same heavy vests shooting Uncle Harry.

She couldn't lose Finn. Not when she and he... She refused to stay down and do nothing while Finn was out there being shot at or, worse, captured. She had to believe nothing bad would happen to him. And where was Tariq? Why hadn't Nick brought him back to the car?

Sophie rolled to her knees and slowly raised her head to look out. The vehicle was surrounded in a dense, smoky fog, nothing like the colored fog used at concerts. She could see nothing through the opaque walls of gray. She crawled to the other window closer to the hangar entrance hoping for a clearer view. As the murky fog encased the car, she was trapped. Her breath caught as claustrophobia closed in. Trying to force air into her constricted throat, she willed herself not to remember.

She couldn't hear Finn or Nick, only a pinging sound hitting the car—the sound of bullets.

The men shooting Uncle Harry, his blood pouring out of his chest onto the cement floor, suddenly flooded her spinning brain. Gooseflesh covered her arms. She bit down hard to stop her body from shaking—the men with their rough hands covering her face with the black cloth, and their coarse Cantonese voices when they threw her on the floor, the strong smell of ginger and anise on their breath. Her heart beat harder, faster. Her palms sweated profusely. She fought the flashbacks. She wouldn't give in to the panic. She wasn't helpless. No black cloth covered her face. She wasn't a prisoner. Taking another deep breath, she consciously tried to slow her speeding heart.

She needed to help Finn, to find Tariq, and get the boy into the SUV away from the gun fight. But Finn had instructed her to stay and if she left, she'd be a distraction for Finn. If she had a weapon, she could protect herself and Tariq while the brothers fought the bad guys.

Grateful for a plan of action, she crawled over the front seat to search the glove box. During the motorcycle chase, she had seen Finn pull a gun out of the glove box. Uncle Harry had taught both Jordan and Sophie how to handle guns and to protect themselves. The glove box was empty. She searched under the passenger seat and then the driver's seat. Her heart was still racing but the panic was contained.

She stayed down despite the fact that she was in a locked, bullet proof SUV. Listening for any sound and whether she should leave the SUV to find Tariq, she realized the bullets had stopped. Total silence except for her harsh breathing. She peered over the windshield toward the hangar entrance.

The smoke was lifting—through the fog she could see the men were running toward the helicopter. Sophie sat up and rubbed her eyes burning from the acrid smoke that seeped into the car not trusting what she saw. A lifeless Tariq was hanging over the arm of one of the men. Her lungs froze. Her heart rate skyrocketed. Her skin crawled with terror.

She unlocked the door and jumped out of the SUV. And screamed, "Stop." Hoping to draw their attention away from Finn who ran ahead of her with a rifle in his hand. The men looked back but didn't stop loading into the helicopter. She sprinted toward Tariq.

"No...No..." She screamed chasing the helicopter, a futile effort as the immense black craft hovered then began its ascent. They took Tariq.

Strong arms wrapped around her from behind. "Sophie." Finn held her against his chest. She fought to break his hold. She wanted to run to the spot where the helicopter had been, to do something—anything—that would stop her from facing...from shattering her world.

"Let me go." Struggling against Finn's chest, trying to fight the constriction of her breathing, the constriction in her heart. "Oh, my God, why did they take Tariq?"

"It makes no sense." Finn sounded bewildered, nothing like the confident SEAL who was always in command of everything and everyone around him.

"This is my fault. I should never have brought him from Nepal where he was safe."

"You brought him because Bunan asked you to." Finn dropped his tight hold and turned her to face him. "Sophie, it's not your fault. I brought this mess to both of you."

Sophie froze with the pain in Finn's voice. Agony was etched across his face, the misery reflecting her own.

Wanting to give into the urge to lash out at someone, to hurt someone like she was hurting, but she couldn't hurt Finn, not when he was suffering, suffering as much as she was. She gently touched his face, a strong, brave face that usually was filled with amusement and teasing. His chiseled jaw was clenched. The blond stubble on his chin, usually sexy, now gave him a dangerous, scary look.

His whole body was tight, holding angry tension. An unrecognizable, enormous, pissed off male loomed over her.

"Only the bad guys are at fault," she whispered. It was strange to be the one reassuring the self-possessed SEAL.

Finn grabbed her hand and pressed it to his lips. "You did great."

She shook her head, trying to avoid Finn's burning intensity. "No, I was terrified. It happened so fast. I couldn't protect Tariq."

She refused to give in to the emotion clogging her throat. "While I was fumbling around, searching for a gun, they took him. If I had gone out sooner..."

He wrapped his arms around her, pressing her against his broad chest. His grip was hard enough to cause bruises, but she didn't care. "And if you had gone out? What then? They'd have you too."

She wrapped her arms around his waist and squeezed tight. They were held together by the pain, somehow making the terrible a bit better. "But he's just a boy."

Finn rubbed his chin along the top of her head. "It wasn't your job to keep Tariq safe. It was mine. And still is mine. I'll find Tariq, and I'm going to make those animals pay."

Finn's ferocity fed her fear and anger. "Terrifying Tariq puts them on my hit list too. I'm going to kill them if I have the chance."

"You're not going to get near these guys. My God, Sophie. I lost you once and today was too Goddamn close." His hand held her in place while he pressed his lips to her.

Sophie anticipated the kiss, expecting demanding and possessive.

Instead, Finn touched her lips gently, his mouth treating her with tender reverence. Sophie leaned close and kissed him back, wanting to reassure this brave man that she could handle whatever he might bring. His hard, taut body joined against her soft, loving strength. Fierce, fearless Finn Jenkins needed her. And she needed him. She always needed him. Forgetting everything but Finn and his mouth on hers, sharing grief, pain, and tenderness in one kiss.

Nick coughed. "We need to get back to HQ pronto."

"Have Jack and Drew follow us." Finn switched gears leaving Sophie trying to grasp if the intimate moment had really happened. He took her elbow and guided her to the back door of the SUV.

Sophie stopped in place. "Are Lars and Sten taking my dad's helicopter to chase them?" Lars and Sten had disappeared once the helicopter ascended.

Finn opened the back door. "By the time they get the helo in the air, those assholes will be long gone."

"But if Reeves tracks the helicopter, can't the FAA stop them?"

"All in the works but helicopters fly low and are hard to track."

Sophie grabbed Finn's arm. "We're going to get them, right?"

"There's no 'we' about it." Finn's hard glare had Sophie backing against the SUV. "I'm going to get them."

"Of course, you are." Sophie allowed Finn to have the last word…for now.

CHAPTER NINETEEN

Finn had to get away from Sophie, away from the fear twisting him like a bowline knot. He mastered tying the knot under water in less than a minute but he wasn't capable of disentangling his emotions from this job. He used the opportunity of Reeves hugging Sophie to slip away to the incident room to do the job that the US Navy had invested millions. Most likely the equation with CJNG would be one Navy SEAL for one Pakistani orphan.

Nick followed him quickly into the room and closed the door, but not before Finn could hear Sten and Lars comforting Sophie. He needed his brothers to keep her away and occupied. Finn had to protect her at all cost despite the hurt coming her way from his rejection. Hurt feelings was a helluva lot better than being in the hands of a brutal drug cartel.

"Before everyone gets involved, you better fill me in about CJNG," Nick demanded. Too many IED blasts and Nick couldn't pass the Marine's Recon hearing test, leaving him adrift after his forced discharge, but yet his brother still missed nothing.

"It's still classified, but let's say that I possibly took out a key man in the CJNG leadership, and they plan to make me and mine suffer."

"How did they get your identity?"

"Exactly. And how did they know to leverage Tariq?"

Nick dropped, sprawling his large body onto the wooden chair.

Nick was the biggest, darkest, and the fiercest of the brothers. A chip off the block of old man Jenkins. "What's our plan?"

"Offer myself up in exchange." Finn paced back and forth in the large room with screens covering every wall. He never wanted to hurt Sophie but today made it very clear. He was a big and present danger to her and he loved her too much to risk her safety.

"I assumed that would be your play. But let's hear the rest?"

The catch was that Finn didn't have "the rest" yet.

"Need to check with the DEA agent who ran point on my last mission to see if he can get any info from his CI embedded deep in the cartel."

Nick kept his dark eyes pinned on Finn. "What else has you jumpy?" This was the real drawback in having your brothers be Special Operators. Couldn't get anything past them. Who was he kidding? He never got anything past his older brother. Finn swallowed the lump in his throat and his ego. "If anything happens to me, you'll take care of Sophie. Don't let her get involved with those jackass, egotistical musicians. She deserves a good man." Finn wasn't going to think about Sophie with another man.

Nick glared. "What the hell are you talking about? My God, has love sapped your brain and your balls? Where is the kickass attitude of *all in; all the time.*"

"I don't need any BUD/s pep talk. Just promise me." It had been awhile since he and Nick had had a real fight, but Finn was in the mood to do damage to someone and he wouldn't mind a bloody brawl. Despite the fact that Nick was Finn's best chance of surviving CJNG.

"You're pathetic. You have to promise me you'll make this up to me with a blonde as hot as Sophie when I'm at your wedding."

Finn wasn't going to wallow in what could have been. And if he were a better man, he'd regret last night but he didn't regret one second of Sophie needing him, Sophie begging him, Sophie taking him to a place he had never been. It was love. Pure and tender. He had been waiting his entire life for last night. It was a memory to sustain him in the long, lonely years ahead. If he lived to get to those years.

"OMG. If I ever act love sick like you're doing right now, you have permission to shoot me."

"One last thing."

Nick ran his hand through his dark, thick hair. "What?"

"You need to run interference with Sophie. She listens to you. I think she's afraid of you. I've got to keep my head in the game."

"SEALs' finest wants me to protect him from one little woman. Sure. Can do." Nick grinned, enjoying his brother's misery. "I'm going to get the twins and Reeves before Daddy Dean gets here."

Nick stood to his six-foot-plus height. "Don't mess up what you have with Sophie. She can be a help. She's a smart woman and she loves you."

Finn stared at the closed door. What the hell? Nick giving advice on women and love. Since when? Finn punched in Lancaster's number. He'd give Dean, his daughter, and Uncle Harry fifteen minutes max before storming the room.

As Finn hung up after hearing nothing but ominous warnings from Lancaster, the door opened and his brothers streamed in. Following them in was Reeves and his IT staff who took their places at the various computer stations.

"Where is Sophie?" Finn didn't want her by herself even if he wasn't able to be the one with her.

"She went up to the apartment to 'freshen' up before her father gets here." A nude Sophie sprawled across the bed upstairs flashed through his mind. Finn fisted his hands until his knuckles ached as he paced in front of the room.

"Reeves, sitrep."

Reeves raised his eyebrows and had the nerve to grin. Okay, Reeves wasn't military but he knew what the hell a sitrep was.

"We're still running background on all the employees at The Heroic Heli School. They have one H130 but it wasn't the one used in today's events. And they know nothing. They did get a call reserving their entire school which was paid in advance and then canceled, which was the reason the school was dark. Terry, who runs the school, gave everyone the day off."

"Can we trace the payment and the phone call?" Sten asked.

"We're on it. And we're tracking all sales or rentals of the helos with no results yet. But it has to be a highly funded organization to have a H130 at its use. We've contacted the FAA but the helo flew low and wasn't tracked. We're waiting on the ballistics of the shots fired."

"They used AR15s. And I doubt ballistics will be of any use," Nick added.

"What about the GPS system in the helo? They have to have used it for their navigation?" Lars didn't sit but stood in the back of the room. Like Finn he needed to be physical when thinking.

"How did they know about your flight? Who on the team knew of the flight plans, Reeves?" Finn asked.

"Only the team. The Jenkins brothers, Jack, Drew, and the pilot, Bill Henderson."

"He's not the leak. Ex-Air Force." Lars laughed. "The crusty airman had his service pistol out and wanted to come out and join the fight. I made him stay in the plane."

"Any of you bozos do any pillow talk last night?" Finn looked between the twins.

"We're not the ones who did pillow talk last night, Finn." Sten waggled his eyebrows.

God, he was going to kill Sten. Did the asshole ever hear of discretion?

"What about your DEA connection? Didn't you talk to him after Conway? Could his phone or his office be bugged?" Nick stared at Finn.

Finn didn't like the hairs on the back of his neck rising. Was it because of his phone calls that CJNG knew of the flight?

"It's a possibility that the DEA office has been compromised. Reeves, look into flights between Jalisco and San Diego. Anyone who has taken frequent flights. And look for four men arriving in Seattle yesterday. I doubt the team that hit us was local."

The only other person Finn called was his CO. Hard to believe that the CO or the Navy's highly secure server was compromised, but then how did the CJNG know his identity?

"Oh, hell." Finn heard Richard Dean's and his uncle's voices. "Keep the CJNG on the down low from Dean until I get a handle on it."

"Wasn't planning to share. But how are you going to keep your night with Sophie off the radar?" Lars asked.

"What the hell are you talking about?"

"Dean will have to be an idiot to not know by the way you're staring at her. It's almost embarrassing to see you in such desperate need. And Dean is not an idiot."

"Shit." The voices of Sophie, Dean, and Uncle Harry grew louder. "Maybe it's easier if I just turn myself over to CJNG right now."

CHAPTER TWENTY

Finn braced himself for the onslaught like the trained military man he was. The door swung open with Dean leading the pack into the room with Uncle Harry, his arms linked with Sophie, following. Dean headed straight to Finn.

"Finn, what the hell is going on? You and Harry assured me that the threat from the Triad was done."

Uncle Harry and Sophie rushed to join in the fracas. Finn, leader of a SEAL team, flipped into control mode. He didn't dare look at Sophie knowing he might do something really stupid like kiss her until they both could pretend this wasn't happening and they would get their happy ever after.

Stepping away from the group, he commanded everyone, including old man Dean. "Everyone, sit down and I'll bring you all up to speed."

Dean's gaze shot between Finn and his uncle.

"Richard, let's hear what Finn and the team have." Uncle Harry took Sophie's elbow, leading her to a chair next to her father.

Dean, in a designer-cut Italian jacket, his gray hair brushed back from his face, hesitated before sitting next to Sophie, but not before glaring at Finn.

Finn looked at his uncle, purposely ignoring both Deans. He had to steel himself against the soft baby blue eyes and the slight scent of Sophie's fragrance lingering in the air.

"Today's abduction of Tariq was a well-planned and well-executed mission. Most likely carried out by hired ex-military mercenaries since they used military-grade smoke grenades, a H130 helo, and heavy firepower without injuring anyone. They fired at our cars and the plane. It was clear their target was Tariq by the way they used the smoke grenades and focused their attack on Sophie to distract all of us from their real goal of taking the boy. Weigh in here, Nick."

"They anticipated that after I positioned Tariq against the SUV to take him out of the line of fire, I'd move to cover Sophie and Finn who were receiving the most fire. It was basic military strategy."

"My God, this is worse than I thought." Dean tugged on his shirt collar as if needing air, a clear emotional tell for the arrogant business mogul. "They were shooting at Sophie? And you weren't able to stop them?"

"That's correct, sir." Finn spread his legs and crossed his arms. He was used to defending his men and their actions to high-ranking military. But if he were in Dean's position, he'd have Finn by the throat for endangering his daughter.

If the mercs had wanted to kill Sophie, they could have. Was this part of CJNG's plan to make Finn suffer by the demonstration they could get to her at any time? Because it was working. Too terribly fucking well.

"They were shooting at Finn too. And Nick, Sten, and Lars. Not just at me, Father."

"But this is their job. That's what I pay them for."

Sophie gasped. "Father, you can't mean that."

"We are all upset by the idea of any of our team at risk, isn't that right, Richard?" Uncle Harry squeezed Sophie's hand.

This was the new relationship between Dean and his uncle since the Dean sisters had been kidnapped. Uncle Harry was helping Dean navigate and repair his relationships with his daughters. "Sophie, you misunderstand. All I meant was that you're not a trained soldier like the Jenkins boys. Of course, I don't want any harm to any of them. They're family."

"But why this boy? What do we know about Tariq?" Uncle Harry asked, drawing the attention away from the uncomfortable silence after Dean's declaration.

"Yes. What does a Pakistani orphan have to do with my daughter?"

"It's the salient question. I see no connection to Sophie except leverage for a ransom. If the reason for the abduction was money, we should receive a call in the next twenty-four hours."

"But who knows about Sophie's relationship with the boy except for our team and the monk?" Sten asked.

Finn's whole body clenched by the unspoken question of who wanted Sophie to suffer by taking the boy. Was it as simple as greed? "That's what we have to find out. Lars, were you able to speak with Bhikshu Bunan?"

"Finn, I wanted to speak with him." Sophie's furrowed forehead and narrowed eyes were exactly like her father, a comparison she wouldn't find positive.

Finn switched his focus back to Lars, stomping down the need to kiss away every one of her lines of frustration.

"He has gone into the mountains for a spiritual retreat and won't be back for three days."

"Convenient..." Dean commented.

"Father, you can't believe such a thing."

Finn shared the same suspicious disposition. The monk's absence was too much of a coincidence.

"Reeves, do you have an update yet on the monk's financials? Any major influx into his account?" Finn didn't need to look at Sophie to know exactly how she was reacting to his inquiries into her beloved monk.

"Why are you investigating Bunan when you know it's the drug cartel who took Tariq?"

"It's important, Sophie, that we look at everyone involved. Finn has to follow every possible lead. He wouldn't be doing his job if he didn't suspect this monk," Uncle Harry added.

Reeves's hands were flying over his keyboard. "His accounts look legitimate—poor, with every donation going into the monastery and the charities. It will take more digging to be sure he hasn't received a payoff."

"The monk has to be the link. He asks you to bring this orphan to the NW and, within three days after you arrive, you were shot at..."

Finn clenched and unclenched his fists at his side, ready to grab Dean and wrinkle his perfectly pressed shirt, and perfectly cut, Italian suit jacket. This wasn't a boardroom discussion where the only thing discussed was loss and profits. This was his daughter and her sensitive feelings.

"Bhikshu Bunan was totally vetted, and his finances examined before Sophie ever became involved with him." Finn glared at Dean, not hiding his hostility for the asshole.

"I did all the research myself." Reeves twisted away from his keyboard to stare at Dean. "But Finn asked me to look for recent deposits."

"I wish I could speak with Bhikshu Bunan and ask more questions about Tariq." Sophie stared at the ceiling, looking lost. Finn wanted to lift her into his arms and carry her away from all the suspicions and ugliness.

"Something you might have done before you brought the boy with you and endangered yourself."

Sophie didn't move but Finn felt her painful internal flinch and, as always, wanted to soothe the sting from her father's insults after he delivered his personal SEAL kind of punishment to Dean. "I'm responsible for the decision to bring Tariq into the states. I vetted him before allowing him on board with your daughter."

"Jesus, Richard," Uncle Harry growled.

Looking abashed was new for the powerful man trying to make amends to his daughters after his shortcomings as a father. "Sophie, I'm sorry. It's just..." His voice broke; the silence in the spacious room was numbing.

He cleared his throat. "If anything happened to you...now that I have you back in my life... None of this is your fault. I know it, but..."

Sophie reached across the table and squeezed his hand. "It's okay. We're all in shock." And there was the reason Finn loved this woman. His glacier-frozen heart was melting by the captivatingly sweet smile she gave her father.

Reeves chimed in, never looking away from his screen. "Tariq has nothing in his background to make him a target. But his background info as a refugee is very sketchy."

"Tariq is an innocent. He wasn't involved until I brought him from Nepal. I'll always be a prime target because of my father."

"Sophie's right. My wealth and power endanger my daughters. Can the abduction of a Pakistani refugee orphan under the care of Richard Dean's daughter who happens to be the organizer of a global summit on the refugee crisis be the reason? A way to embarrass me and my family?"

Finn's mind went into a tailspin. Was he totally off base? Could it be possible that his association with CJNG wasn't the reason for the abduction? If the CJNG wanted him by the balls, wouldn't they have killed Sophie or one of his brothers, not abduct a Pakistani orphan? He should feel relief that he might not be on CJNG's death list but Sophie was still in the middle of the mess.

"It would mean the press would bring back all my past escapades." Finn hated how Sophie's face paled and she twisted her hands on the table. "I should cancel. My appearance would take away from the plight of refugees and turn the important conference into a media circus." She gave a rueful laugh. "And I was worried about appearing with Alex. What a joke."

Was this some elaborate plan to embarrass Dean? The team would need to look again at all of Dean's enemies. The damn summit put Sophie right into the crosshairs of CJNG or whoever was behind Tariq's kidnapping. "I agree with Sophie. We should cancel everyone's appearances at the conference."

Finn stared at Sophie, willing her to understand he'd do anything to protect her. "Not because of the press coverage but because of the unknown threat."

"My father and Jordan shouldn't suffer because of me. I'll cancel."

"No one is canceling." Dean reached and touched Sophie's hand. "We're a family and we'll handle the press and any threat being thrown at us. Finn, you have three days to figure out who is behind this."

Finn opened his mouth, but Uncle Harry gave Finn the high sign not to respond.

"We can make the decision about the conference when we get closer. We have to wait for the ransom demands." Finn pretended his heart wasn't racing and his palms weren't sweaty from the rush of adrenaline pounding through his bloodstream.

Suddenly the door blasted open, and Jordan, red hair flying, swooped into the room. Aiden, her behemoth fiancé, also an ex-Delta Force operator, followed behind.

Sophie jumped up and hugged her sister. Both started crying and talking across each other.

"Oh, my God. We got here as fast as we could." Jordan wiped away the tears from Sophie's eyes as Sophie kissed her sister's cheek.

All the men were transfixed by the open display of emotions between the sisters. Not easy for Alpha males who didn't express feelings since they barely acknowledged their existence.

"Who is behind this?" Jordan, with her arm wrapped around Sophie's shoulder, demanded of Finn.

"It's the drug cartel that almost killed Finn in his last mission." Sophie rushed before Finn could answer.

"He's going to do something stupid. Jordan, you and Father have to talk him out of it."

All eyes were on Finn now.

Aiden, standing behind Jordan, smirked. "Something stupid, huh? Sounds about right."

"Thanks for the vote of confidence." Finn stopped himself from calling Aiden a jackass.

CHAPTER TWENTY-ONE

Assuming the final pose of her yoga routine, Sophie stretched flat on her back into the savasana position also known as the "corpse pose." She inhaled, focusing on her breath and not the irony of the pose's name. The passive pose was more challenging than the active poses because it required a release of the mental chatter and a surrender into a state of presence.

Despite her disciplined practice, she couldn't stop her brain from spinning in circles of what-if. Her mind ricocheted between Tariq and Finn. It had been two days since Tariq had been abducted with no clear leads and no ransom call. Sophie's own abduction experience left little to her imagination with the terror Tariq was living in. Her breath froze and fear blasted through every cell with the vision of Tariq bound, terrified, and alone with no one able to explain what was happening to him.

Sophie consciously inhaled for the count of three and exhaled for the same focusing on detaching. Who was she kidding? Detachment? All she could think of was Finn and what twisted labyrinth of suffering he was imposing on himself.

In his Alpha-macho thinking, he was convinced that she was in danger because of him. He blamed himself for the gun chase, the kidnapping, and the shootout at the airport. Knowing Finn's over-exaggerated sense of responsibility and control, he probably blamed himself for today's rain and who was the president.

The man was usually a master of logic and control but how did he think that avoiding her was a way of protecting her? At first, she believed he was busy when he never came upstairs and he didn't come to bed. In some warped way he believed he had to distance himself.

The light tap on the door had Sophie jumping from the mat hoping for good news. "Sophie. I'm back."

Unlike Sophie who was forbidden to leave the apartment, Jordan, with Aiden as her bodyguard and a four-person detail, was allowed to go to her genetics lab to check her specimens.

After hugging Sophie, Jordan held her at arm's length to inspect her face. "Were you able to nap?" Both sisters had stayed up last night until the early morning hours, rehashing everything about Tariq, and the suppressed fears that resurfaced about their own kidnappings—despite that the sisters had escaped their captors.

"Have you eaten anything?"

"The idea of food…"

Jordan wrinkled her nose. "When you were missing, I couldn't eat or sleep."

"I never appreciated how difficult it must have been on you. The waiting…the unknown…worry."

"It wasn't the terror you went through. And I had Finn and Aiden doing their best to console me."

Jordan grabbed Sophie's hand and led her into the spacious modern living/dining room. "Let's get you something to eat."

Seeing the crumpled blankets where Finn had slept last night halted her step. She held tight to her sister's hand to help ground herself. Was she the crazy one here? She understood that he needed time to come to grips with the kidnapping and their night together but that he chose to sleep on the couch instead of with her was intolerable. The stupid man made the wrong choice. Sophie planned to help him make the right choice.

"How come you had both Finn and Aiden? And all I get is Laurel and Hardy?" Sophie coaxed a smile out of her somber older sister who always worried about her baby sister. Finn had sent his brothers to console Sophie and give her updates. She knew how bizarre the situation was getting when Nick, the man who made fierce Viking-like Aiden, look soft and cuddly, came last night for a heart-to-heart.

"I've never seen Finn like this." Jordan opened the refrigerator and sorted through containers of food. "Yogurt with fruit? French toast?" Bent over the refrigerator, Jordan lifted and inspected the marked containers from the kitchen staff. "He's worse than when you were kidnapped. He is completely shut down, robot-like."

"He's blaming himself despite the fact that we have no clues about who kidnapped Tariq."

"I think fearless Finn is scared by the intensity of how he feels."

"I'm trying to give him space but I'm not sure it's the right idea."

"He needs to get his shit together." Tough love from Jordan was new. "Aiden is bringing him up here so you two can talk."

"Finn won't come." Last night, Sophie had considered going downstairs to confront Finn. Normally she didn't mind making a scene, but she didn't want to announce their relationship in a public and dramatic way.

"Oh, yes, he will. I promised Aiden..." Jordan's green eyes sparkled with her wide grin. "Never mind what I promised Aiden, but, trust me, Aiden will make Finn come. Aiden said he would carry Finn if Finn resisted."

"This should be entertaining."

Sophie plopped on the couch, wrapping herself in the blankets in hopes of getting the scent of Finn. "It's a bit humbling after being considered one of the most eligible single women in Seattle Magazine that my sister has to trade her favors to get me a guy."

"Sharing my 'favors' isn't too difficult with Aiden." Jordan tittered like a teenaged girl. Love had truly changed her uptight, science-nerd sister.

"I can imagine." Sophie clasped her hand over her mouth. "Forget it. I don't want to imagine."

The sisters started to laugh as the door swung open.

Aiden held the door for Finn who rolled his eyes at his close friend as he entered the apartment. Sophie wanted to jump off the couch and wrap her arms around him. He looked exhausted, his eyes were red-rimmed, his color wan, and his stubble was thicker and darker, making him look both dangerous and sex incarnate. Heat moved up her body with the memory of the marks on her thighs from his beard when he...Sophie's heart went into double-time.

Finn didn't meet her eyes but spoke to Jordan. "Really, Jordan? You sent your fiancé to strong-arm me—as if he could."

Neither Sophie nor Jordan chose to comment with Finn nearby.

Aiden held his hand out to Jordan. Sophie watched her sister chew on her lower lip, the same habit as Sophie. Jordan's porcelain skin flushed a bright pink. The sexual tension between the two was rapier sharp. Aiden's harsh breath filled the silent space.

"Really, Aiden. You don't have to be so obvious." Sophie heard her sister whisper as Aiden dragged Jordan behind him toward the bedroom.

Sophie felt like a voyeur, embarrassed to be privy to her older sister, a mother figure, about to get down and do the dirty.

Sophie looked up to see Finn watching her with the same hungry need as Aiden had for Jordan. Caught in the sensual stare, Sophie couldn't look away, her whole body leaning toward him and the promise in his burning eyes.

Aiden turned back from the doorway to glare at Finn. "Do not think about interrupting us. Any attempt and you'll regret it." He shut the door and the turn of the lock echoed in the tense room.

"Why would I want...?" Finn shook his head, running his hand through his disheveled hair.

"What did Aiden do to get you to come upstairs?"

"He said he'd owe me big time if I came upstairs. He hinted that Jordan had promised to make him a very happy man."

"That's it? He didn't threaten you?"

"Like he could?" Finn stood by the dining room table not moving closer. "He exaggerated his 'prowess' for Jordan's benefit."

"Of all the low tricks."

"I don't think Jordan will mind. Do you?"

Sophie patted the seat next to her. "Finn, come. Sit down. You need to take a break."

His eyes flashed as ruddy patches moved across his cheeks. Recognizing Finn's arousal, Sophie felt the heat and need soar through her body. She wanted to lead him to their bedroom in the same masterful way Aiden had taken Jordan.

"Soph, I need to get back to the incident room."

"You can sit down for five minutes and give me an update." Sophie was afraid he truly might leave.

"Five minutes."

Sophie had to restrain herself and not roll her eyes. And she might have if Finn didn't look so exhausted and vulnerable. As SEAL commander he was used to controlling his world and his emotions. Without the control, he looked as lost as he had after his father's death.

Finn lowered himself two cushions away from Sophie.

"Just talk to me. Tell me what's going on in that complicated brain of yours." She'd have to muster all her patience because all she wanted to do was strip the man naked and offer sweaty primitive comfort. "What are you thinking?"

"Thinking?" His angular chin jutted out, the pulse in his neck throbbing, his erection bulging against his jeans.

"Are you still working with the theory that the cartel took Tariq because of your last mission?"

"I never agreed with your idea."

"From all that you didn't say, I think I'm right."

"It is one of our working theories. But it seems less likely that it's revenge. If the cartel was involved, they would have demanded something by now." He ran his fingers through his sandy blond hair, causing it to spike, and all she could think of was the way she'd gripped his hair when his head was between her legs.

"And all your background checks and everything the guys have been running didn't come up with anything?"

"Nothing. Which makes the possibility that the kidnapping has to do with your father more salient. Bhikshu Bunan is clean as you already knew. I'm sorry, Sophie, but you have to understand the reasons I had to investigate him."

"I spoke with Bhikshu Bunan. He was very upset to hear about Tariq. And I understand you had to do your job. My only issue is why you're avoiding me."

"I haven't been avoiding you. I've been doing my job. Tonight, is the opening party for the summit."

Searching for forbearance, Sophie counted backwards from ten in Farsi.

"You've been working nonstop for two days. And you don't have time to talk to the woman you love?"

"God, Soph. That's why I've waited...and I shouldn't have. Your feelings were hurt that I was investigating the monk. I do worse things than suspect holy monks of trouble."

"Finn, you protect people and our country. I respect you and the work you do. I always will."

"My work brought really evil men into your world." The hopelessness in Finn's voice unnerved Sophie.

"I was kidnapped by the Triad because of my sister's genetic research. And you don't know that Tariq's kidnapping is related to your work." Sophie inched closer and rested her hand on his taut, muscular thigh in his worn blue jeans. "Does that mean Jordan should avoid me? And you should avoid me?"

"You're talking apples and oranges. My work is all about taking risks, walking into danger not away from it. And it's all-consuming. I have to be focused and always in total control to protect my guys. If I'm distracted... I might make a mistake. Men's lives depend on me. And right now, your life and my brothers' lives depend on me making critical decisions. You're going out in public in a few hours." He ran his hands through his hair, making more spikes, staring straight ahead. "Our night together was a..."

"Don't you dare say it, Finn." Sophie, never known for her patience, lost it. She turned on the couch facing Finn and poked him in his broad, taut chest. "And why do you get to decide, huh?

I don't get a choice? There were two of us in that bed together. Both sharing our feelings."

"Because you're gorgeous, smart, the hot, sexy Sophie Dean. You don't need a man who brings you heartbreak and danger."

Sophie poked him again, not that it had any effect on the wall of steel, but it felt good to touch him. How could this man who had women panting with a mere smile, a man who was loyal, brave, and trustworthy, not know how much she loved him? "You're going to bring me heartbreak? You're not going to be faithful?"

Finn lifted her finger and rested her hand on top of his thigh, his hot, calloused hand pressing hers. "My God, Soph. How can you ask? Why would I ever stray when I have you in my bed?"

"Then what are we talking about here."

"I can't protect you at the conference if I'm thinking of you naked—all soft and open, wanting me."

"That's the reason you let me be alone in that bed after our night together?"

"Sophie, I can't let anything happen to you again. Now that you're mine. Truly mine. I don't think I could live..."

Sophie grabbed his hands between hers. "You don't think I'm not afraid? Afraid that something could happen to you. You just said it—you like walking, if not running, into danger. But that isn't going to stop me from loving you. I need you, Finn. I need to be in your arms. I need to offer you comfort and receive comfort in return. You know withdrawing from me feels like my dad. When he couldn't handle his grief, he left Jordan and me on our own."

"I've been an idiot." He lifted her from the couch onto his lap and wrapped her arms around his neck. "All I could think about was that I needed to stay far away and focus on getting the bastards before your appearance at the summit."

"You get to be an idiot if you make it up to me right now."

Finn's rumble laugh vibrated through her, his erection pushing against her. She flexed her hips, enjoying the way Finn's light skin reddened and his broad chest heaved.

"Forget drug cartels. You're the one who is going to be the

death of me, Sophie Dean." He lifted her yoga shirt off of her exposing her red exercise bra.

"Did I tell you how much I love your breasts?" His fingers circled her nipple.

Mesmerized and breathless, Sophie, watched Finn's absorption with her breast, the careful way he circled her nipple, bringing it to a pucker.

"You might have mentioned it." Eager for more, Sophie leaned forward, wanting his mouth on her now. She licked a path along his neck, scattering love bites before she flicked her tongue into his ear.

Sophie felt Finn shudder when she sucked on his neck.

He lifted her breasts into both hands and squeezed.

Needing his mouth on her, she reached to stretch the bra over her head but Finn had other ideas. He lowered the bra beneath her breasts forcing them upward to give him free access. "I never knew how much I love this kind of bra." His tongue stroked the sensitive nipple. Sophie couldn't stop her hips from riding his hard shaft.

"I need you inside me right now. Let's go to the bedroom." Sophie moved back and forth against Finn, her yoga pants a thin barrier to his hard length. Then she felt a vibration and his "Beast of Burden" ringtone. Lost in sensation, she kept moving. She was about to dry hump herself into an orgasm.

"Of all the timing. I'm going to kill Reeves." Finn lifted Sophie off his lap and placed her next to him on the couch, trailing his calloused finger along her nipple before he started to struggle to pull his phone out of his jeans pocket. His engorged member stretched his jeans tight. "Damn, Sophie. See what you do to me."

She stared at Finn, trying to catch up with the interruption. Every nerve ending edging toward release. "Finn," she begged, pushing her breast against his hand as she rubbed her hand along his length, wanting to put her lips around him, watching his eyes widen in need.

"Stop, woman. I need to answer this."

Sophie giggled as Finn stood up and jiggled his man parts before being able to reach into his pocket.

Reeves's voice reverberated in the room. "What the hell, Finn? Why aren't you answering your phone? We were about to send the team up." Then Sophie could hear laughter in the background.

"Very funny. And tell my brothers to stop fucking around, I still can kick every one of their asses."

By her position on the couch, she was eye level with Finn's erection. Her female parts purred in anticipation. Her heart sped with her burning need to have Finn deep inside her, their bodies joined, moving together.

"I'll be right down. Start looking at security and the street cameras around the area." Finn flipped into his measured commander voice.

Sophie reached to grab Finn's arm. "No, Finn. You can't leave me like this."

"Trust me I don't want to leave you." He growled before he knelt in front of the couch. "Soph, I'll be back as soon as I can." His knuckles purposefully rubbed along her breasts as he pulled up her bra to cover her.

"Finn Jenkins. You better have a damn good reason why you're leaving me high and dry."

Finn's ruddy cheeks made his eyes shine brighter. He traced one finger down the seam of her tight yoga pants, teasing her. "Dry? Soph, you know that you're soaking wet if the other night..."

Sophie scooted closer, wanting his touch, wanting to yank down her pants, to have his fingers inside her. "Please, Finn, let's go to the bedroom. We can be quick."

Finn lifted her off the couch, holding her tight against him, her feet off the ground, her sensitive nipples stroking across his chest. "We are never going to be quick. And when I make love to you, darlin', there is not going to be anything quick about it. Except how fast I can get you off." Possessiveness raged cross the harsh planes of his face as his lips hovered just over hers.

"Promises, promises." Sophie nipped his full, plump, lower lip while she clung, pressing her body against him, wrapping her legs around his waist wanting to keep the contact.

His mouth crushed hers, and she let out a savage moan as the heat and need sizzled across her skin. He tasted like sex and sin and she opened her mouth wider to taste his wild hunger.

Finn leaned back to look at her. "See how easy you distract me, Soph. Uncle Harry is downstairs. His men have found the helicopter in an abandoned warehouse."

Her burning needs vanished in a nanosecond. Sophie dropped her legs to the floor. "Tariq?" Her pulsating heart thudded hard against her chest. "He's been found?" The words choked out around the fear.

Finn brushed the hair from her eyes, his touch lingering behind her sensitive ear lobe. "No. I'm sorry. The building is empty but Reeves might find something on the cameras."

Relief made her knees shaky and she leaned into Finn for support.

"This might be the lead we were hoping for. These guys were pros, so I don't want to get your hopes up."

"I'm coming downstairs." She grabbed his arm. "Waiting with nothing to do is killing me."

"I know it's been hard on you. It's going to be over soon." Finn checked his watch. "But don't you have to get ready for the cocktail party?"

Sophie moaned aloud. How could she have forgotten so quickly that tonight was the social event for the speakers and donors, the event she worked on for months? Because Finn made her forget everything.

Since a ransom demand hadn't come in, they were moving to the second possible reason behind the kidnapping. Tariq's kidnapping was intended to embarrass her father at the summit, a political ploy on the global stage of the wealthy and powerful.

"No, let's stick to our plan. You're going to appear in public as if nothing has happened. This might be the time the kidnappers make contact with you or your father. We don't have anything else without a ransom demand. The security is locked down tight. Nothing is going to happen to you this time. This won't be like Hong Kong. I'll kill anyone who tries, including Alex Hardy if he pulls any moves."

"Very funny." Sophie chose not to mention at this moment that Alex was texting her, but Reeves was monitoring her phone and most likely reporting it to Finn.

"You think I'm kidding? I was restrained in Nepal because I thought you cared about him. But now, all bets are off."

Sophie scooted next to Finn and ran her fingers along his day beard. "Your jealousy is pretty hot. But I'm not worried about my safety. I'm worried about Tariq. He's been with them for almost two days."

"He's a resilient little guy. He traveled from Pakistan and lived in a refugee camp. But there is one thing you can do to help the team."

Finn's lively eyes got the familiar mischievous gleam that always spelled trouble for the Dean sisters. A devious look that should have warned her.

"Tell Aiden I need him downstairs. ASAP." With a brief buss on her lips, Finn was out the door. She could hear his laughter echoing from the hallway.

CHAPTER TWENTY-TWO

Finn adjusted himself trying to alleviate the pressure on his bulging jones from his jeans zipper. Just what he didn't want was to go downstairs with a raging hard-on. His brothers would never stop giving him shit.

He took the steps two at a time down to the main floor. He needed to shut down the sensation of Sophie's breasts filling his hands and the mewling sounds she made when he fingered her nipples. With Sophie in the mix his million-dollar training at compartmentalizing was losing the battle. He had been a fool trying to keep his distance from Sophie. He just made both of them miserable.

Uncle Harry, looking fit and energetic after his bullet wound, leaned against the wall outside the incident room, waiting for Finn.

"Is Sophie better today?"

Was this some universal joke? Neither he nor Sophie were better and wouldn't be until they were back in bed. Finn kicked at the scuff mark on the floor to avoid his uncle's probing stare, feeling like a teenager caught red-handed.

"When I had dinner with her last night, she was pretty upset by how you've been behaving. Not that she would criticize you. I thought I raised you better than needing Aiden's threats to man up."

"My brothers have big mouths."

"Yes, they do."

"You damn well know that I'm not intimidated by anyone. I

went along because Jordan was upset enough to send Aiden."

His uncle barked out a deep-throated laugh. "Now that's a whopper. You boys have always underestimated the Dean girls. Sophie isn't going to fall apart. You need to give her credit for being able to handle what gets thrown at her."

"I don't underestimate Sophie. I just give CJNG credit for being merciless, vicious, sick fucks."

Finn squirmed under his uncle's silence. Uncle Harry was a straight in-your-face kind of guy who never held back in voicing his opinions. "What's this chat really about?" An awful dread seeped into Finn. "Tariq is dead?"

"No. I just wanted to make sure you don't do some dumbass shit because your head isn't screwed on right," Uncle Harry rumbled before opening the door.

"Thanks. I guess." Finn spoke to his uncle's back as he followed into the incident room.

His brothers were slouching in their chairs while Reeves and his crew were typing on their keyboards as their screens flashed with code. The mood was somber. None of the brothers commented on his arrival or bantered their usual trash talk. After his uncle's warnings and the unusual restraint from Reeves and his brothers, the silence was eerie and weirding him out.

"Start talking, Reeves." Finn never thought he'd ever make that request to the perpetually wired Reeves.

"The security cameras around the building were scrubbed but I was able to enhance them."

Finn waited. His muscles clenched and he felt the spike in his pulse and tried to not grind his teeth. How bad could it be? By the solemn mood in the room—Armageddon. No one spewing wisecracks and no physical threats between his crew, was more unsettling than Finn realized. What could be on the screen that had silenced this macho crew?

Had Tariq, a sweet, small boy, been tortured? He wouldn't put it past the sadistic CJNG. Like all the men in the room, Finn had witnessed a lot of horrendous shit buried deep in the deep recesses of his memory.

"I never got any images of the mercs, only this guy, and, when I ran it through facial recog, he comes up DEA."

Finn stared at the blurred image of DEA agent Todd Lancaster standing in front of the wooden doors of the warehouse, talking on a cell phone.

Rage and shock railed in Finn. Nothing prepared him for the deep betrayal. Lancaster was the mole. An America federal agent betrayed his country and Finn's SEAL team. Finn's team. His other brothers. And caused pain and incredible suffering for Sophie.

"I'm fucking going to kill him."

The door flew open with a resounding bang as the door smashed against the wall. "This better be important." Aiden spoke through his clenched teeth. "Or there is going to be bloodshed." He stopped mid-room when no one reacted, then grabbed the chair next to Uncle Harry.

"Nothing I despise more than a traitor," Nick growled. "Reeves, is there any way you can track his phone?"

All random thoughts and reactions crystallized into one mission—revenge. Finn's body ramped into a killing zone. He was a predator on the hunt.

Reeves never stopped typing. "Ye of little faith. I already triangulated his position with the cell towers and then used an algorithm to get his number."

"The guy is deep in shit balancing the cartel and DEA. He's using burners." Sten's legs were stretched out in front of him as he leaned against the back of his chair, but it was all an act. The men in this room dedicated their lives to protecting the innocent and defending their country. "No way are we going to get him with his phone. He's dumped that phone by now."

Aiden's deep voice resonated in the room. "What are we dealing with?"

"We don't know anything about him. Classified except that he's DEA from Finn's last covert mission. The photo was taken in front of the warehouse where the helo was found."

"And one *Mexican Commando* is dead because of this slimy bastard." Finn ground his teeth instead of punching the wall.

Dark, heavy silence descended on the room like the fog that blanketed Seattle. Nothing put good men into a rage more than a fellow officer sworn to duty turned traitor.

"Let's nail his ass." Aiden stared at Lancaster's image.

"We have to find him first. He has to keep using the same phone for us to get a read on his GPS." Sten was an IT guy too. "And the footage is from yesterday morning."

"But if he's making contact with whomever wanted Tariq, he might be using the same phone," Lars added. "Keeping one phone for the cartel business."

"We've got to face that the kid might already be dead. It's going on thirty four hours and no ransom call." Uncle Harry looked at Finn, his rigid military bearing softened by his familiar gruff voice.

"He killed a kid to draw out Finn?" Lars jumped out of his seat to pace in the back of the room.

"You think this is a trap. Not a mistake to be caught in front of the cameras?" Sten asked.

Every instinct ingrained in Finn's body was standing up and shouting, "Hell, yes!"

"This isn't personal," Uncle Harry warned. The only reasonable voice among the killing revenge escalating in the room. "You need to report this to your CO."

"Feels personal. He used an innocent kid and Sophie." Finn wouldn't report to his CO until he had Tariq and Lancaster in custody. He wouldn't kill Lancaster. That would be too easy. Nothing like going to prison with the men you put behind bars.

Uncle Harry didn't make a sound but Finn could sense his disapproval from the ten feet separating them.

"I've got the sucker." A female voice came from behind one of the computer screens. "The number from the burner was just used. There is a possibility that he tossed it and someone else is using."

All the male eyes turned to the only woman in the room full of raging, bristling testosterone.

"Nice work, Izzy." Reeves winked at the inked woman, her raven black hair in a messy ponytail, matched her entire black outfit. Elizabeth Benson aka "Izzy," a Stanford dropout who had never uttered a word in Finn's presence before today.

Izzy kept typing, ignoring the men's stares or Reeves's acknowledgment.

"Bring up the address, Izzy. Let's get a look at where he's hiding." Finn's heart pumped with the adrenaline surge while his breathing smoothed out. His body knew the drill of seek and kill.

"It's Burien—just south of West Seattle." The giant screen showed a wooden sixties ramshackle house with two black SUVs parked in front.

"This is where they're holding Tariq." Finn always trusted his gut. "Let's go, guys. Suit up."

"Finn, this is your operation, but shouldn't there be more time for an assault plan?" Uncle Harry stood. "And what about Sophie's private detail for tonight's event?"

Finn checked his watch. He had two hours before the party, plenty of time to accomplish his mission. "Lars and Aiden will cover Sophie until I get back. Sten and Nick are with me. And I'll take the rest of our first team I've had on-call." Since Hong Kong, Finn had been hiring men from his Spec-Ops connections to be available for the dangerous jobs, upping the training and skill of the entire security team.

"I'll cover Sophie's security, but you better be the one to tell her about the change." Aiden leveled Finn with one of his *I-can-kill-you-with-one-blow* looks which as usual had no effect.

"Not enough time. And if she finds out we have a lead on Tariq, she'll demand to be part of the operation. Chances are this is a trap. And no way in hell I'm allowing her to walk into a trap." He didn't mention that he didn't want Sophie to see the brutal savagery pounding through him. He wanted to protect her witnessing him as the trained killer he was.

"He's letting you be the one to walk into a trap." Lars elbowed Sten who now stood in the back of the room. "I told you I was the favorite. Older brother stuff. I'll be eating caviar and checking out the hot women while you're fighting those mercs."

"Who doesn't like a trap? Where's the fun in a basic assault?" Sten shoved back. "You're getting soft in your old age." Lars was two minutes older than Sten and the arguments never stopped.

"You won't survive to have caviar or hot women, if you let anything happen to Sophie." Finn stormed to the door. "You hear me, little brother?"

Lars, of course, had to have the last word. "I'm not your little brother. I'm bigger than you are."

Working with his brothers often felt like working in a psych unit. But they had his back. And Finn never doubted that Lars would die protecting Sophie.

CHAPTER TWENTY-THREE

Gulam leaned back against the leather couch to enjoy the "smoky peat" flavor of his Dalmore Scotch while Asif and his men swept the hotel suite for surveillance bugs possibly planted by his friends at the CIA or his Kenyan rivals who were trying to take over his African route.

The dense, gray fog cloaked his expansive view of Puget Sound. Seattle's wet and dreary climate was exactly like London—the dampness collected in your bones, making them ache, unlike the sweltering heat of his homeland.

Gulam watched the men move through the expansive, four-bedroom suite. Richard Dean, the ultra-wealthy owner of the hotel, had the entire top floor for the conference. His net worth rivaled Dean's but it was sheltered away from public and government eyes.

"Are they almost finished?" Gulam spent millions in counter-surveillance equipment, most recently purchasing the latest white noise emitter which prevented laser eavesdropping. Otherwise, his enemies might beam a laser at the window and listen to the conversation transmitted by the vibrations of the glass.

Asif escorted the guards to the door. "It is safe to speak now."

Gulam nodded at his cousin who stood before him waiting for permission to sit.

Unlike Gulam, Asif didn't relax against the pillows but sat upright, his highly polished, black shoes planted squarely in front of him. "I just received word that our package is on the way. They were awaiting your arrival and should be here shortly. Finally, we can tie up loose ends."

Despite the risk of allowing Tariq to live, his nephew was Gulam's only male relative, the only rightful heir to inherit the business. Unless one of his daughters married a man he could trust. Gulam was still undecided on Tariq's fate once the boy was back in Pakistan.

"They're bringing him into the hotel with the NGO organizations who are setting up displays in the exhibition halls. He is drugged and inside a large trunk."

"You and only you will see to his well-being. No one is to enter his room. I want no harm to befall him while in the United States. We are only here for image-making. It is circumstantial this other business has occurred."

"Of course. And the cartel wanted you to be informed that abducting Tariq had much higher risks than first anticipated."

"They'll get no more money." Gulam tightened his grip on the crystal glass. "And tell them of my great irritation for trying to manipulate me."

"They don't want any money. But they want you to feel indebted for the risk they've taken on your behalf."

"And what is the fucking big risk of abducting a Pakistani orphan?"

"Richard Dean's younger daughter is the one who brought Tariq out of Nepal."

Suddenly the Scotch didn't bring the comfort that soothed his throat and heated his chilled body. "Why would Richard Dean's daughter bring Tariq to the States?" There it was again, the jittery sensation spiking down his spine. He stretched out his legs on the ottoman in front of him, assuming a relaxed position while he battled with control. "How did they gain this information?"

"Their high-placed informant used his connections to dig deeper into the blonde in the car with the SEAL. The SEAL is friends with the Dean family and was acting as a bodyguard."

"How dare this woman, a mere woman, interfere with my family? My business. I'd like to…" His jaw ticked from the pressure of holding his rage tight.

"She is speaking tomorrow on the worldwide refugee crisis. Maybe Tariq was to be an example of her generosity. Americans like to display their humanitarian side."

Fury whipped through Gulam. His highly respected lineage was to be trotted out like one his ponies on the world stage to be pitied and under the mercy of a stupid American woman. And if anyone found out that Tariq was his nephew, questions would be raised. Questions he never planned to answer. How dare this woman? First Yasra and now Dean's daughter. He'd like to teach Dean's daughter her place in the world.

"I never like when you get that look on your face." Asif shifted on the couch. "It always involves risk to my life."

"I pay you damn well to take risks." Gulam swirled the amber liquid in his mouth, enjoying the burst of flavor and heat. "And what I'm thinking is that it is going to be a pleasure to meet this blonde woman. I will make a very generous offer to her refugee cause."

He loved the irony that he'd receive UK tax breaks for his charitable donations to the refugee crisis that fueled his business of human trafficking. On recommendations of his financial advisor, he diversified his portfolio two years ago. Drugs would always be the best investment, but trafficking had an exceedingly high profit margin because humans could be sold over and over again.

"How will she be able to resist my magnanimous efforts?"

CHAPTER TWENTY-FOUR

Sophie chewed her lower lip trying to ignore the anxiety crawling under her skin as she waited to get the all-clear from Lars and Aiden before joining the cocktail party. Where was Finn? He promised to be here.

Cold, eerie fog blanketing Puget Sound crept through the ceiling-to-floor windows of the reception room. From the doorway, she scanned the crowded, brightly lit room—attractive women in cocktail dresses, men in designer suits, wait staff in the standard black shirts and black pants handing out appetizers and hors d'oeuvres from silver trays. Nothing different than thousands of similar events she had attended.

Nothing different except her heart thrashed against her chest and her hands were sweaty—sweaty palms like the teenage boys who used to try to feel her up. Nothing different except Lars and Aiden were behaving as if this was a Spec-Ops mission. Tsunami waves of tension exuded off the hyper-vigilant men. The wait staff, with their broad shoulders and bulging necks and biceps, all looked like pissed-off NFL defensive players who happened to be carrying weapons. And Finn was MIA.

"I can't wait to describe this to Sten," Lars quipped, staring at two blonde, voluptuous women in killer high-heels, and barely covering, tight cocktail dresses. The donor guests made a sharp contrast to the NGO workers and volunteers who wore nothing from the haute couture collection or carried designer purses and had shoes that cost more than their monthly salary.

"Yes, sir. I'm able to multi-task. United States Marine Corps has trained me well," Lars spoke into his mic to Aiden.

Lars stood at Sophie's left to enable her access to her weapon. She clasped her small cloth Versace purse which contained a Ruger LCR. Nothing she owned met the requirements of appropriate cocktail accessory and the ability to conceal a handgun. Lars instructed her how to shoot through her Versace bag, to simply put the lightweight compact revolver in her hand, finger on the trigger and shoot.

It would be ironic if jokester Lars was kidding.

Alex, having just arrived in Seattle, stood at the bar with several women clinging to him—nothing new as he grinned and basked in their adoration.

Though once Alex spotted Sophie at the door, he was on the move. His shiny ebony hair was down and whipping across his shoulders as in some hair shampoo commercial. The charismatic man did know how to work the crowd. She could almost hear everyone sighing in awe of his physical grace and beauty. But her heart belonged to rough-and-tumble Finn Jenkins who would never work a crowd the way Alex did unless moving as part of a SWAT team did it for you.

"Oh, hell. Finn told me Alex is not to touch you or he'll make me suffer in ways I don't want to imagine. And with you in that do-me get-up, I'm going to die." Lars moved next to Sophie.

"For your information, my dress is not any different than any other woman here. In fact, I'd say my Alexander McQueen is quite conservative. That seems like a non-sequitur. And Finn should be here if he wanted to get all possessive."

"Listen, Soph. We already went over this…"

"I know. Finn is in pursuit of a possibly dangerous lead to Tariq. Someone Finn worked with betrayed him." It was possible that Finn was being shot at right now by those same scary men who attacked them at the airport. And she was helpless to do anything. Was this going to be her future life with Finn? Never knowing where he was or who was shooting at him. Never knowing if he would come home. Fear jammed into her throat making it difficult to draw air.

"He could have taken the time to explain the situation." Worry spiked her words with a bite she hadn't intended.

"He didn't have time if he wanted to make it back for this party."

"My point exactly. He didn't make it to the party and didn't explain." Wow. Love did make her sound like a bitch. But containing her anxiety about Finn and the pressure of the summit was taking a toll.

"He couldn't disclose because it is classified. None of us know what his mission was. It's the way Spec-Ops roll and it's the way you're going to have to roll if you stay with Finn."

Sophie put her hands on her hips and glared at Lars. "Why wouldn't I stay with Finn? I love him." Maybe Finn was right. Maybe she didn't have the cojones to handle a SEAL's life. And what about when they had children? Her anxiety was edging to panic.

"Well, you are pissed off with the guy, and he's just doing his job."

"No wonder you don't have a woman in your life. It's called communication, Lars." It was a lot easier to take out her frustration on Lars than admit to any doubts.

Lars held up his hands. "Don't shoot the messenger. Finn will be here. But until he's here, I'm in charge. So, don't let Alex Hardy touch you."

"You're in charge of my security. Not in charge of me. Got that straight?"

Lars chuckled. "Aiden just said you sound like your sister."

Sophie ignored Lars and walked to the middle of the room to greet Alex, aware that all eyes were on them. There would be no publicity from this event, and most of the people here could care less about tabloid news, but, still, she didn't want the attention on her. This was about getting the one percent of the one percent to invest their money in humanity.

Alex swept her into his arms and would have kissed her on the lips if she hadn't averted her face. "Alex, please."

Lars grabbed Alex's arm. "She said stop, asshole." Lars, five inches taller and fifty pounds of muscle heavier than Alex was an impressive site, though impressive wasn't what she wanted in the middle of her event where she didn't want any drama. "Lars, go away."

She pulled her arm out of Lars's grasp, and took Alex's elbow to lead him away from the center of the room and center of attention. "I'm sorry for my bodyguard. He's taking his job way too serious." She said it loud enough for Lars to hear.

"I'm right here and not going anywhere."

Alex brushed the hair from his eyes with is practiced gesture. "I understand. Any man in your sphere wants to protect you from all comers."

Once again she counted backward in Farsi. It was typical of male thinking to believe that being guarded like a favorite bone was a compliment to a woman. "I grew up with these men and they see me as their kid sister."

Alex leaned close to her ear as Sophie felt Lars protectively looming behind her, as a bulky man approached from her right.

"May I be bold enough to introduce myself?" Sophie turned to the dark, smooth, complex voice that was like a shot of Dos Lunas Grand Reservea with the taste of almonds, coffee, oak and sherry all blasting your tongue.

His tailored black suit, open-collar, blue, silk shirt, and a gold chain around his neck shouted foreign wealth. His black hair and eyes, his olive skin, and British accent, branded him as a subject from one of Britain's ex-colonies. Sophie loved guessing accents, but she needed him to speak more to determine his roots.

"Please join us." Sophie paused, wracking her brain for his name. In prep for the summit, she had repeatedly gone over the guest list during the long hours in the apartment. His appearance matched the description of Gulam Khara, the CEO of the London-Dubai import company. Her father had no business with Mr. Khara that she knew of. His acceptance of the invitation to the philanthropic refugee summit was somewhat of a surprise since he was not known on the global stage for donating or championing a cause.

"I'm Sophie Dean. And this is Alex Hardy. Alex also is very devoted to the refugee plight, Mr. Khara."

Alex's full lower lip, admired by women over the world, stuck out in a pout by being forced to give up Sophie's attention. And men referred to women as high maintenance.

"No introduction is needed, Miss Dean. Your reputation for compassion for refugees precedes you. I've read your *New York Times* article on the crisis in Syria. It was very thoughtful and part of the reason I decided to attend this conference. Please call me Gulam. My native country also struggles with the plight of refugees."

Sophie, recognizing his enunciation of vowels, answered in Punjabi that she was very aware of the high number of Afghan refugees in Pakistan and India.

"You speak Punjabi?"

Sophie liked seeing the shock on the arrogant man's face. His eyes were calculating and despite his conversation focused on refugees she was quite adept at reading his subtext of sexual predator on the make. He had undressed her with his eyes in the first seconds of meeting her.

"You speak with a perfect intonation. Not many non-Pakistanis can do that." His hand glided along her bare arm, giving her shivers of the creepy kind that all women learned to recognize.

"Sophie is very skilled in many languages." Alex crowded closer. "She was able to discern the various dialects of the refugees that we worked with in Nepal."

"I did see the photos of your visit, Mr. Hardy. Not many stars of your caliber and heiresses of large fortunes are willing to give their time to the problems of poor, uneducated masses."

Was it just a coincidence that Tariq was from Pakistan and Mr. Khara? Might this just be the connection they were hoping for? Except the summit had been planned long before Sophie had met Tariq and brought him from Nepal, and Mr. Khara had been on the list for months. She was desperate, chasing shadows.

"Thank you, Alex." Sophie smiled. "I've always been interested in languages. What part of Pakistan are you from Mr. Khara?" She refused to call him by his first name, avoiding further intimacy.

"I'm originally from Lahore." His heavy lids shuttered down hiding any reaction she might see.

Suspicion skittering along her nerve endings, Sophie shifted back on her favorite black Louboutins.

"Lahore?" Alex wrapped his arm around Sophie's shoulder. "Sophie is very skilled in the Lahore dialect. In fact…"

Before Alex could mention Tariq, Lars asked, "Do you want me to get you a drink, Ms. Dean?"

Mr. Khara's ultra-white, veneered teeth flashed. "Your bodyguards are much more attentive than mine. I'm never offered drinks. But with your beauty who can blame them?"

"I have very diligent bodyguards, Mr. Khara."

"I'll leave you to your much-admiring company, Miss Dean." He lifted Sophie's hand and pressed his damp lips to her hand. "I'd be honored if you'd join me later in my suite for a drink. I'd like to speak in my native language. It's been awhile since I've been home. And I'm most interested in your ideas for the solution of the refugee crisis."

"Thank you for the invitation, Mr. Khara. I'd love to speak with you but I believe Alex has exaggerated my proficiency." Sophie controlled the urge to wipe her hand on her dress to remove his touch. And hell would have to freeze over before Sophie met this man in his suite to "speak his native tongue." His interest wasn't in refugees or as a possible link to Tariq. She knew what he was interested in. She had learned sleaze radar by the time she was sixteen and Mr. Khara topped the charts.

CHAPTER TWENTY-FIVE

Slipping away from Alex, who had been waylaid by several eager fans, Sophie moved toward the windows, away from the crowd gathered at the bar. She worked to bring this assembled impressive group of people together and she wasn't going to allow Lars, Alex, and one slimy Pakistani to distract her. Tonight's goal was to bring the donors and the experts together to begin the dialogue for the summit.

She searched the room for Dr. Josh Harrison, tomorrow's keynote speaker. In a well-worn, outdated, tweed jacket and wrinkled khaki pants, the unassuming social science researcher from the Stanford Immigration Policy Lab and delegate to the United Nations High Commission for Refugees stood by himself.

"Dr. Harrison, welcome to Seattle." Sophie offered her hand. "I hope you had an easy trip."

"Please, Sophie, call me Josh. And you found me in the corner observing like the crusty scientist that I am. By the guests you've assembled, this is going to move the conversation forward. Congratulations, you've done a bang-up job."

Sophie's face flushed to the tops of her ears at the compliments from the humble humanitarian she admired. "Thank you. The summit was the work of many."

"But you were the only one to bring all the players together. Your voice and leadership will make a difference in building bridges between the various organizations. I hope you will continue to do this work."

Looking around, Sophie could feel the lively energy in anticipation from the prestigious guests for the summit. She didn't take credit for the overwhelming response. She was aware that her family name drew the crowd. There hadn't been a lot of time to think about taking the position with the foundation. Tonight though was confirmation that she could use her family name and family money to make a difference. And despite her trepidation, she was ready to take on the challenges ahead...including Navy SEAL Finn Jenkins.

"How is your sister and her research?"

Jordan had introduced Sophie to her professor after Sophie had become particularly interested in the conditions and issues confronting women refugees.

"She will be here tomorrow for your speech and hopes you'll have time to catch up." Jordan was not happy about Aiden and the team nixing her appearance tonight but the team saw her appearance and their father's as an unnecessary risk. This was Sophie's summit, and no one could stop her from attending.

Sophie's phone vibrated. "Please excuse me." Her pulse zipped into a loop-de-loop. It must be Finn. He would call her if they found Tariq. She moved away from Josh, closer to the door.

Bhikshu Bunan spoke rapidly and it took a minute to follow his Nepalese. Tariq's aunt had arrived in Kathmandu. Sophie's hands shook and her knees wobbled as she listened to Bhikshu Bunan convey that Gulam Khara was Tariq's uncle and was responsible for Tariq's kidnapping and the murder of Tariq's family.

What Bunan had just revealed was hard to process. Then Tariq's aunt came on the phone and pleaded with Sophie to find Tariq and prevent her brother from leaving with him. In shock, Sophie braced herself against the wall to keep herself upright, having trouble processing that that smarmy Mr. Khara was that sweet boy's uncle.

Suddenly Lars was next to her. "What is it, Sophie?"

"Not here." Sophie hooked Lars's arm and led him into the lobby. Fierce anger palpated off Lars when Sophie delivered the information about Tariq.

"He blew up his father, his brother and his family." Sophie shuddered. "I see him at the bar. I'm going up to his suite to look for Tariq."

Lars grabbed her arm. "You can't go up there by yourself."

"I'm not planning on it. You and Aiden will be with me. And you better get a hold of Finn wherever he is and tell him to get over here."

Sophie's voice quivered with false bravado. She trusted Lars and Aiden, but she needed Finn. Where was the blasted man? He better not get himself injured when she needed him.

"Damn it, Soph. We need to coordinate with Reeves and the team."

"I'll go over to him and make the arrangements to come later to his suite."

"But he'll want you to leave with him now. I saw how the perv was checking you out."

"I'll say I have to stay with my guests, but will join him for a nightcap to give you time to get everything ready."

"Why does Sten always get the better gigs?"

"Thanks a lot, Lars." Sophie couldn't believe Lars accepted her plan so readily. Finn was going to be a whole different game.

Sophie read the surprise on Khara's face when she approached him at the bar and proposed a drink. This wasn't not how she saw this long-anticipated night playing out. She watched the bartender mix her drink before he handed it to her. Her clubbing experience had taught her to never blindly accept a drink.

"Ms. Dean. How lovely that you can join me. You've completed your hostess duties?"

Sophie gritted her teeth from responding to his condescending comment. She switched to the Lahore dialect. "No, I still must see to the guests. But I never can resist practicing my language skills. There were people from Lahore in the refugee camp."

He leaned his elbow on the bar, angling his body toward her.

"You met refugees from Lahore? How interesting. Were there any children from Lahore at the camp? I'm appalled to read about the conditions in the camps, especially for the children."

Sophie's stomach was jumping like the "shoot"—the newest dance move at the clubs. "No children." She gazed directly at him. She had no trouble standing her ground with her father, Richard Dean, one of the world's most powerful men. Khara was easy-peasy when she thought about Tariq and what this man made the boy suffer.

A man reaching for his drink jostled Sophie and she was pushed closer to Khara who was looking down her dress.

She took a slow sip of her drink, making sure to lick her lips, liking the way his breath caught, and his face suffused with color. "What brought you to the summit, Mr. Khara?"

The candlelight from the bar flickered in his dark eyes. "I'd love if we could take this conversation upstairs."

Fear skated across her skin. Khara somehow knew of her connection to Tariq. She read it in the gleam in his eyes and the mocking tone in his voice. He was enjoying the cat and mouse game, with him as the big bad cat. Sophie had a surprise for him. She was no dumb, blonde mouse.

"Sophie, when can you leave?" Alex came up behind her. "I was hoping you and I could go over my notes for my talk tomorrow?"

Sophie couldn't blame Alex for his assumption that they would spend time together. There hadn't been an opportunity to talk, but now was not the time. "I've been practicing my Punjabi with Mr. Khara."

Alex was looking back and forth between them trying to get a read when she heard Danni from across the room.

"Soph. I'm sorry I'm late but my Uber driver took the longest route to get here." Danni's deep, sexy voice had both men turning and then staring at her progress through the crowd in the ultra-short, zigzag Missoni dress and high wedges showcasing her tanned legs. Her long hair was pulled up and her chandelier earrings swayed in time with her hips.

"Danni." Sophie hugged her friend, trying to not show her surprise. She didn't need to look at Lars to know that he wasn't reacting well to her girlfriend's appearance.

Danni leaned down and whispered into her ear. "Jordan sent me as backup since Aiden was being a big asshole."

"Thank you for coming." Sophie used their closeness to murmur. "You need to go home."

"No way would I miss your big night. I'm here for moral support."

If Danni only knew.

"Oh, my." Danni peeked from beneath her outrageously long and mascaraed eyelashes. "You're Alex Hardy. I didn't realize you were going to be here tonight or I would have taken a cab instead of Uber."

"This is my dear friend Danni." Sophie purposefully didn't give her last name, not wanting Khara to know anything about her friend.

"Danni, this is Mr. Gulam Khara who is visiting from London or is it Dubai? Your company has offices in both cities if I remember right."

"You're very knowledgeable, Miss Dean, about my company. I reside mostly in London."

"I've tried to learn as much as I can about the attendees of the summit."

"It is a pleasure to meet you, Miss Danni. May I get you a drink?"

Danni crowded in between Sophie and Khara. Bless BFFs who read male problems and had the wherewithal to bail you out.

"Will you excuse me? I see that Dr. Harrison is leaving." Sophie wasn't worried about Danni being able to handle herself with either man as long as Danni stayed at the bar. Keeping two men on the hook was baby's play for the beautiful and brilliant woman.

"Miss Sophie, can you still join me in my suite later? And I hope Miss Danni can join too? And, of course, you Mr. Hardy."

"I'd be delighted to join you, but I'm sure Alex and Danni have other plans. I do need to bring my bodyguard. My father insists that he never leaves my side."

"As a father of four daughters, I understand your father's protectiveness."

"I've no plans, and I'd love to join you." Danni's full magenta lips curled up. Of course, Danni wasn't going to leave. Jordan had clearly told Danni to stick to her side. She didn't need Danni to have another traumatic experience because of the Dean sisters.

"I hope you won't keep me long, ladies. I've just arrived and am suffering from jet lag." The edge to his suave British accent didn't hide the threat.

Sophie walked to Dr. Harrison who was talking with Letitia Albright from Oxfam who was on a panel on the inherent poverty of refugees. Lars followed behind Sophie as expected to give her the opportunity to devise their plan.

"Why in hell did you invite that woman?"

Sophie kept walking, talking over her shoulder. "I didn't invite her and she just invited herself to the suite. So, you need to deal with it. Do you and Aiden have a plan?"

Sophie stopped to thank two of the guests knowing that Khara was watching her every move.

Lars showed Sophie his watch as if they were on a schedule. "Finn is almost here and wants you to wait."

A rush of relief shot through with the news of Finn's safety. "Did he get any information?"

"None."

Sophie turned back to smile at Danni and Khara. Alex handed his phone to a laughing Danni.

"Oh, my God. She's going to hook up with Hardy. She's giving him her number." Lars was throwing icy daggers at Danni.

"I think Khara knows."

"Knows what?"

"That I'm on to him. He pointedly asked me if I met any children from Lahore."

"Finn, did you hear that?"

Sophie grabbed Lars's arm. "Finn, can hear us talking?"

"He's on comms now and on his way here. And the edited version is that you are not to go anywhere near the suite."

"But how will I find Tariq? He must be in Khara's suite."

Sophie's brain was churning as she walked toward Dr. Harrison who was leaving. "It's the only way to get information from him. Finn, I need to go the suite."

Lars rubbed the back of his neck. "I feel as if I'm schizophrenic having a conversation with two people in my head."

"Well, next time, Finn Jenkins, I should have an earpiece. Did you hear that?" Sophie moved toward Dr. Harrison, but didn't miss Lars rolling his eyes upward. It didn't take much of an imagination to guess Finn's response.

CHAPTER TWENTY-SIX

Finn clenched the steering wheel as he sped to Seattle's waterfront and Sophie. What was she thinking going to a hotel suite with a known murderer and a kidnapper who was in bed with the drug cartel? Tariq's abduction was organized by Todd Lancaster who was on CJNG's payroll. Today was turning into a monster clusterfuck.

He was too late to get to Tariq and now he was late to protect Sophie from her half-baked, crazy-ass plan. He liked well-planned and well-prepared operations with trained men who followed his orders.

"Don't make me kill you, little brother." Finn's pulse hammered against his chest as he accelerated across the West Seattle Bridge, yelling into his mic.

"Just get your ass here. The crowd is thinning out and it's going to be hard for Sophie to keep stalling him."

A FUBAR. No question that Sophie's idea was more than the military expression of fucked up beyond all recognition. Finn swerved the SUV around the gridlock on the bridge merging to the entrance to North I-5 while those waiting honked at him for cutting them off.

"I should have driven." Sten gripped the overhead bar on the passenger side as Finn drove onto the shoulder to pass the backup on the highway.

"Do not let Sophie near that devil." Finn had to consider the possibility this was some sort of elaborate plan to kidnap Sophie by the drug cartel.

"Aiden, sitrep."

"We're in position to storm the suite. No one is posted outside the door."

"Execute." Adrenaline pulsed through Finn's veins as he listened to Aiden and the men shout "clear" as they swept Khara's suite.

"Nothing here. No electronics. No sign of the boy." At the Burien house where the lowlifes held Tariq, there had been ropes tied to the bed frame and fast-food wrappers scattered on the floor.

Finn dodged cars to take the Seneca Street exit, having to drive on the shoulder again to pass the congestion.

"Planting the bugs then we're out of here," Aiden said.

"Shit. Wouldn't Lancaster take Tariq to Khara? Reeves, have you been able to track the SUV? We need to know where they were headed."

"Oh hell—why is she here?" Lars moaned into the mic. "A goatfuck."

"If Jordan is there, I'm going to blister her backside." Aiden growled.

"Worse... Danni."

Sten laughed. "Well, hell and damn."

"Lars, cover Danni until I get down there." Aiden's sigh came loud and clear over the mic. "If anything happens to Jordan's friend..."

"I going to kill Khara, he just patted Danni's ass."

"Get in line, little brother." Finn turned onto Alaskan Way. "It might help to have Danni as a distraction and a way to stall Khara. We're five minutes out. Keep them in the bar."

"Oh, hell, one of Khara's men has pulled him aside. I'm heading over."

"Keep comms lines open. And don't allow Sophie to go anywhere."

Finn went into mission zone as he pulled the car into the fire lane in front of the hotel and threw the car into park.

Sten took off his ear mic and grabbed Finn's arm. "You can't go in there and set off Khara. We can't raise his suspicions if we want to get the boy back."

"I know what my mission is, asshole. Until Sophie is away from Khara, all bets are off."

"Jackass. Sophie will never forgive you if you go all Rambo and lose the chance to find Tariq. Or worse, get him killed."

Sten was right. He was a royal jackass. He left Sophie for revenge and for some misguided heroic notion that he had to be the one to rescue Tariq. And now the woman he loved was right smack in middle of danger. From an operational point of view, he could argue he made the right call. But Aiden, an ex-tier one operator, could have organized the assault on the house. And right now Finn would be with Sophie preventing her from getting herself killed. Blind dizzy panic rolled over him. She'd better wait for him or he'd never... What? Never forgive her?

CHAPTER TWENTY-SEVEN

After bidding Dr. Harrison good night, Sophie moved toward Danni and Khara who were crossing the nearly empty reception room.

The evil man held Danni's arm in a tight grip with a sick, sweet smile. Danni leaned her weight on the opposite hip with an attitude of "whatever" but her wide dilated pupils, pinched lips registered her fear.

"If you don't want Tariq to die, you and your friend will join me in my suite. All I need to do is raise my hand and you see that tall gentleman by the elevator, he'll send the message to Tariq's guards. He's such a good boy. I'm sure you wouldn't want the death of a child on your white, American soul."

She tottered backward as if she had been viciously struck. She sucked in the pain and terror. "You've decided to finally give up the act of the humanitarian?"

"And you haven't given up your act as an interfering bitch with too much money." Khara pushed closer. His nostrils flared on his broad nose. His impenetrable black eyes narrowed before Lars crowded on her left ready to step in front of her. "I just discovered that my suite was searched."

Sophie gave a fake snigger. Her brain scrambled for solutions while her heart slammed in agonizing jabs against her chest and her hands and legs shook. If they didn't go with him, he would kill Tariq. She had to detain him until Finn arrived. "Hate to break it to you, but you're not the first to accuse me of being a bitch or having too much money."

"Why am I not shocked?" Khara nodded to the man standing outside the door. "Time is running out. Your life for Tariq's. If you refuse…" He shrugged nonchalantly. "It's very easy to arrange the death of an American woman involved with an Ahmadi infidel by an extremist Pakistani."

"Let Danni go. She has nothing to do with any of this. I'll go to the suite with you. Whatever you want, but let her go."

"Oh, but she now is part of it. Aren't you, darling?" Tilting his head back, Khara slowly perused Danni from her legs up to her chest where his eyes lingered.

Danni put one hand on her hip as if she were enjoying being looked over like a slab of beef. "Hey, I'm in for whatever entertainment Mr. Khara has to offer. It's been a slow week."

"Goddamn it, Danni." Lars repositioned between the two women.

"The devoted watchdog. Are you the Navy SEAL that I've been hearing about?"

The wild and reckless need to break into a run thumped in Sophie's brain over and over. When it came down to it, she preferred flight over stay and fight.

Any of the guests watching the interaction would have no idea that this was anything but a friendly chat. Lars had an earpiece so Finn and the men knew what was going on. She didn't know military strategy, but they like her, must be weighing the threat of Tariq's murder.

"I'm going with the women." Lars widened his stance as if he was ready to attack Khara despite the hulky guy with soulless eyes behind Khara.

"I expected as much. Of course, the more the merrier." Khara gestured with his arms for Sophie to go ahead of him to the elevator doors.

Sophie linked arms with Danni after Khara released her. Lars walked behind both women.

"Jordan owes me big." Danni winked down at Sophie as they

stepped into the elevator. Since Danni's breakup with her fiancé and the kidnapping, she had developed a definite nihilistic attitude. Sophie was going to call Danni out—once they escaped.

They rode in silence with Khara and his bodyguard to the twenty-fourth floor. Another bulky guard stood at Khara's suite door.

Sophie hesitated before crossing the threshold when she spotted another bodyguard with his weapon drawn waiting in the expansive room. "This is insane. You'll never get away with whatever you have planned. My father will hunt you down if anything happens to me."

"I've gotten away with a lot more than the death of one rich, meddling woman. This is all your fault bringing my nephew to the United States." He waved his arm for them to move further into the suite. "Your reputation as a party girl precedes you. And I can't wait to read the headlines. Rich girl parties with her bodyguard and friend at global summit. But I'll be long gone with Tariq by the time you and your friends are found."

The controlled tension pounding off Lars was seeping into Sophie. She had to keep Khara talking. She had to keep it together until Finn and the team arrived.

"Asif, get the drugs. We haven't much time. In your partying days, did you try a speedball? My ephedrine factory in India is expanding into the production of fentanyl. Dealers on the street are cutting the meth and cocaine with fentanyl. Supposedly you get quite a euphoric high if you don't die of overdose."

Terror crashed into her chest. Her breathing erratic and wild. Aware of every sound, every movement, she felt the subtle shift in Lars when Asif returned with the syringes. Panic prickled along her spine. She could smell the fear. She had to get it together. Something terrible must have happened to Finn or he would've been here. She had to save Tariq.

"Danni, do you remember our time in Federal Way?" Sophie was confident that Danni would understand the reference to when they assaulted their kidnappers to escape.

"We sure did party that night, didn't we?"

While Khara leered at Danni who was moving her hips shaking to a beat in her head, Sophie surreptitiously opened her purse, reaching for the Ruger. Her hands trembled when she put her finger on the trigger.

"I'm sorry that I don't have time to join your little party," Khara rubbed his obvious erection as he stared at Danni.

Without any hesitation, Lars pulled out his weapon and shot the two-armed guards. Sophie raised her purse and fired at Asif. Her shot went wide as Asif kept moving, syringes in one hand, with a malevolent look that made her entire being squirm.

In a blur of motion, Danni kicked Khara in the head, sending him crashing to the floor.

Asif, raised his gun and aimed at Danni. Lars dove in front of her, taking her to the ground while firing at Asif. Lars hit Asif in the chest.

Quickly scrambling to his feet, Khara rushed Sophie who raised her purse to fire again but Khara grabbed her and wrapped his arm around her neck with one hand and taking a knife out his jacket with the other, placed it against her neck.

CHAPTER TWENTY-EIGHT

Finn jumped out of the SUV and ran to his team assembled in the lobby for the assault on the suite. Shouting commands, Finn went into the zone. If he allowed any emotion, like the insane paralyzing fear, to slip out of the steel box, he'd have already ordered an assault on Khara at the reception despite the risk of casualties and potentially Tariq's murder.

Seth, a retired SEAL operator, was trying to herd the crowd back into the reception area.

Finn ignored the stares of the guests who milled around despite the presence of eleven armed men in full-body armor. "Team one—take the front stairs. Team two—service elevator. Aiden, Sten with me—front elevator."

The men raced away.

"Reeves, talk to me. I've lost contact with Lars."

"I had them in the hallway, but, once they entered the suite, I lost them."

Finn stepped into the elevator that Sten held for him. "How the fuck did you lose them?" Adrenaline was mainlining into his veins. He couldn't level out his heart rate or his breathing.

"They must be using a jammer."

"We didn't find a jammer when we swept the room," Aiden said.

"It could be portable and brought to the room after the sweep."

Finn punched the elevator button. He needed to see Sophie

right now. God, in the three minutes since she went with Khara to the suite and the time for them take over the suite…anything could happen. He closed his speeding thoughts as his training kicked in.

"Reeves, take over this elevator. No stops."

Aiden and Sten stood by him with their AR15's ready, pointed at the elevator door.

Finn watched the panel as they ascended. Fourteen floors to go. His entire body clenched in readiness to kill anyone standing between him and Sophie.

Suddenly, the elevator jarred and stopped.

"Reeves, what the hell? Get this running." Finn's brain was going to explode.

"They've taken control of the elevators. We're working on it."

Finn wasn't waiting. "Let's do this."

Thank God, this was one of Seattle's older waterfront hotels or they would have been trapped. He pulled out the stop button, pressed on the push bar on the side of the elevator then knelt on the floor positioned to insert his fingers in the tiny crack between the closed doors. "If they're controlling the elevator, they're waiting for us on the other side."

Aiden knelt next to him to assist in prying the doors apart to about an inch opening.

Finn motioned to Sten to stand to the side by the panel as he stood on the opposite side. "Sten, cover Aiden."

On his knees, Aiden had his rifle in his right hand, his left hand on the gap between the doors.

"On my count." Finn pointed his gun at the center of the door. "Three, two, one."

Aiden nodded as he pulled the door open a foot—enough space to get off rounds. Two men with their guns at the ready waited. Finn and Sten fired. Aiden rolled and shot one as Finn took out the guy on his side.

Holding their defensive position, Finn and Sten waited for Aiden to stand then Sten helped Aiden finish prying the door open. As they emerged from the elevator, Finn took point, with Sten next, and Aiden covering their backs.

Todd Lancaster, in full-body armor, came around the corner. At the sight of him, Finn exploded into revengeful killing fury. He blasted the traitor with a perfect kill shot to the forehead, but not before the asshole scored a hit off Finn's vest. The pain was immediate and searing, but Finn kept moving to Lancaster's prone body. Lancaster stared up at Finn before becoming vacant. Finn kicked the gun away from Lancaster's limp hand.

"You okay, bro?" Sten stepped next to him.

"Great. Let's get the hell upstairs."

Finn signaled for Sten to go first to the stairwell at the end of the hallway.

"They'll be waiting for us in the stairwell. The perfect kill zone."

Finn and Aiden stood on each side of the doorway while Sten opened the door. Finn rushed behind his brother to cover the upstairs while Aiden covered the downstairs.

Aware of every sound, Finn gave the signal to ascend.

Sten pointed upward at the base of the stairwell, scanning the area as they waited in the soundless space. "It's empty."

"Arrogant bastards thought they had us at the elevator. I was hoping for a little more action." Aiden chuckled. Nothing like rolling with D Force.

"Reeves, sitrep."

"Elevator is working but Lars's comms is still down."

"We're getting on at the eleventh floor. Make sure it works or I'm going to kick your ass."

"Roger that, sir."

Finn stepped out first on the twenty-fourth floor. He wouldn't be stopped when Sophie was with the killer. One heavy bodyguard, at the door to Khara's suite, raised his rifle, but Sten burned the guy.

Silently, they took positions on each side of the door. Finn kicked in the door. He was coming in hot and heavy, ready to obliterate anyone on his way to Sophie. With Sten and Aiden covering him, he rushed in.

His relief at seeing Sophie alive vanished by the sight of Khara, holding a khukuri, a Middle East machete, to Sophie's pale neck. Her pupils were dilated and her carotid was pulsating, but she managed a brief smile.

"You're late."

The sight of Finn emboldened Sophie. Nothing could go wrong. Finn was here.

"We had a little trouble with the elevator." Finn's eyes did a sweep of her and then the scene in the room. "How do you get yourself into these situations?"

She tried for a smile but knew Finn saw her bloody terror.

Sten and Aiden followed Finn into the room with their rifles drawn. And all now pointed at Khara, the only one left standing. She knew it wouldn't matter how many guns they fired at Khara, it would only take one swipe... She tried to pull away but Khara just tightened his grip.

"It's over, Khara. Let her go." Finn's eyes never wavered from her face.

"It's over for the meddling bitch." Khara pressed the cold metal deeper against her throat.

Sophie's heart was thumping so hard it felt like it would jump out of her chest. She looked at Finn, knowing he'd do his SEAL mojo. "I love you, Finn. Never loved anyone else."

Khara laughed. And just like Uncle Harry taught her, Sophie stomped her stiletto heel into his foot and then dropped to the ground when Khara loosened his grip.

Finn shot Khara. The thud of his body resounded in her ears as his body fell next to her. She scrambled away, not wanting to look at the dead man. Finn lifted her into his arms to take her away from Khara who stared up at her with a hole in his forehead. She closed her eyes trying to shut out the horrific scene of the dead bodies in the room.

Squeezing her tight, Finn spit out in a raspy voice, "I'm going to go to my grave with the image of that asshole's knife on your neck."

"I knew you would shoot him. Knew you wouldn't miss."

Sophie leaned against the hard strength of Finn's heaving chest, trying to stop shaking.

"Oh, my God. Lars is bleeding," Danni shouted, trying to rip her dress and finally yanking the Missoni over her head.

"I would have gotten shot sooner to get your dress off," Lars moaned as she pressed the designer dress to his bleeding thigh.

Sten rushed to Lars and knelt and felt for his pulse. Aiden ran out of the suite but his words echoed into the silent room. "Lars is down. Single gunshot wound to his leg."

"You, asshole. You were probably checking Danni out instead of doing your job." But Sten's voice cracked as he took over applying the pressure.

"He dove in front of the bullet to stop it. He saved my life." Danni cried, tears rushing down her face, kneeling over Lars in her red lace bra and panties.

Finn carried Sophie outside the suite into the hallway where men she didn't recognize stood guard with rifles. "I need to check on Lars and then I'm getting you the hell away from here."

Although she didn't want to go back into the suite with the scattered bodies, she wasn't abandoning Lars. "I'm not leaving Lars. And once we know Lars is okay. We have to find Tariq. He has to be in the hotel, because..." The words came out around a sob. "Khara said he'd give men the signal to kill Tariq if I didn't go with him."

"I know, honey." He gently kissed her on the lips. "I heard. Don't think about it. Men are sweeping the hotel. It won't be long before he's found."

"I had to go with Khara. I tried to let Danni leave... I couldn't let anything happen to Tariq."

"You did the right thing. None of this was your fault. This was all my fault. I should have never left you."

Sophie's lashes lifted, treating him to the sight of her dazed violet eyes. "Finn, you couldn't have anticipated this scenario. No one could have."

He brushed her hair away from her face. "Honey, it's my job to anticipate the worst. That is what I'm trained for."

Her lips parted into a small smile. "There is definitely something wrong with your training, if you think saving me, Danni, and Lars wasn't good enough."

"Is that right, honey?"

"And when Tariq is found, we're going to celebrate what a hero you are."

He pulled her into his arms. "Nope. We're going to celebrate my kickass heroine."

CHAPTER TWENTY-NINE

Finn tracked Sophie's movement back and forth on the deep plush rug in her father's hotel penthouse. He finally got her to leave the gory scene once Lars was taken by ambulance. Her tight black-patterned dress was covered in Khara's blood, her hair was half up and half down, tumbling around her shoulders, her eye makeup smeared from her tears. She never looked more beautiful to him.

"Are you trying to make me feel better after everything that has happened? Do you really believe Tariq is in the hotel?"

"Reeves found the footage of the mercs arriving at the hotel's service entrance with a large trunk."

"Oh, my God." She halted and grabbed her heart. "They put him in a trunk? He must have been so frightened."

Finn wanted to hold her and reassure her but she was still riding on the adrenaline high. "He's going to be fine."

"How do you know?" By the way she stood with her hands on her jutted-out hips, worrying her lower lip, Finn reached flashpoint. He had to touch her. He stepped to close the space between them. Unaware of his desperate need, she turned and strode back across the expansive space.

"He's just a boy. And he's been through so much upheaval."

"Do you know why he's going to be fine? Because he has Sophie Dean on his side."

She stopped pacing and rewarded him with the sweetest smile. "Tariq is in the hotel. We'll find him."

"I don't understand why Reeves can't find Khara's room registrations." With the shake of her head, more hair fell down around her shoulders. And what kind of man did that make him that all he thought about was releasing her hair from its confines and...

She kicked off her heels on the last path across the room. "Shouldn't Lars be at the hospital by now? Jordan and Uncle Harry are on their way to Harborview. Jordan said she'd call me once she had news."

"The bullet didn't hit a bone or major blood vessel. He's going to be pissed that he'll be put on leave from MARSOC, but Danni's heartfelt gratitude will help his pain." Finn didn't want to think about how sideways tonight could've gone while he was fighting Lancaster and his men.

Sophie snickered in a brittle tone. "Can you believe Danni, in a hotel bathrobe, was arguing with Sten on who got to ride in the ambulance?"

"Honey, come here." Finn opened his arms. "Why don't you jump into the shower and get cleaned up? It might help you unwind before you see Tariq."

Sophie wrapped her arms around him, pushing her soft body against his, her voice low and silky. "Don't you want to unwind with me?"

The raging erection that he had been sporting since Sophie dropped to the ground to give him a clear shot at Khara just got harder, although he didn't believe that was physically possible. Sophie Dean, ballsy and caring all mixed into a hot bod was finally his. He didn't deserve her, but he didn't care. She was his. And only his. The most basic primitive need to get her alone and naked after watching the bastard hold a knife to her neck was driving him despite all the chaos around them. "Nothing I'd like more...but..."

"I know. We haven't time. Once this is all over. Promise me, Finn Jenkins, that you and I are going to Orcas Island and, no matter what happens, we will not get out of bed for days."

Finn lifted her against him. "Yes, ma'am. After today's threat,

I'm not letting you out of my sight." Not exactly the way he planned to make his declaration.

Sophie's bright eyes were darkened by her arousal, her voice ragged with need. "I feel the same way, Finn."

God, if he didn't have to go downstairs and deal with the Seattle police, FBI, DEA, and his US Navy, what he would do...

His phone rang. "They found Tariq. He's been in a room on the sixth floor and wants to see you. Aiden is bringing him now."

"Oh, thank God." Tears pooled in her eyes.

Finn tenderly kissed her forehead as he smoothed her hair. "You better get out of that dress before you see Tariq. I had the men bring some clothes from your room."

"You did? You know you're pretty amazing?"

"I'm going to remind you when you're pissed at me." He slapped her on that soft ass. "Get moving, Soph."

She laughed over her shoulder. "Payback is hell, Finn."

"That's what I'm praying for."

Sophie was back in the living room before he had finished drinking the glass of water he poured himself from the fancy water dispenser. How she changed out of her clothes and into her yoga outfit in less than five minutes was hard to imagine. But then he didn't want to imagine—Sophie naked squeezing herself into the tight, red sports bra.

She rushed right past him with the knock on the door and swung the door wide open. Tariq, in the same clothes from his abduction at the airport, ran into Sophie's open arms. Sophie crooned in a soft voice, reassuring him in Punjabi that he was safe and that his Aunt Yasra was on her way.

Finn watched the unlikely pair—the vivacious, blonde woman with blue eyes and the dark boy with black eyes. The joy emanating between them caused a lump to form in Finn's throat. He was one damn lucky man to have a loving, spirited woman like Sophie in his life.

The chatter between the two stopped, and Finn caught Tariq eyeing his full-body armor complete with his gun holstered at his side.

Finn knelt on one knee to lessen the imposing figure he made to the small, frightened boy. Tariq didn't hesitate and ran right into Finn's arms, trying to get his slender arms around Finn's middle. "You saved me."

And for the first time since his father's funeral, Finn felt the sting behind his eyes. He looked up to be captured in the most loving look from Sophie. "You'll never have to worry about your uncle hurting you again. I'll always protect you."

Then Finn lifted Tariq off his feet to swing him in the air. "Are you hungry? I bet Sophie can whip something up for you while I have to attend to some business."

"Payback, Finn Jenkins."

"Promises. Promises." Finn echoed Sophie's words.

Sophie took Tariq's hand. "Let's go see what's in the refrigerator."

With his hand on the doorknob, Finn turned. "I'll be back later for my payback, Soph."

CHAPTER THIRTY

Six bloody hours to deal with the alphabet agencies when all he wanted was to be naked with Sophie. And next week he'd have to fly to San Diego to deal with the fallout of Lancaster, the traitorous bastard. Finn nodded to Seth, standing at the door to the penthouse, then opened the door with the electronic key.

At 3 a.m., the penthouse was totally silent as expected. All he wanted, after finding Tariq, was Sophie, to comfort her in the way of male comfort after her harrowing day. Instead he had to explain himself first to the police, then the FBI and then the fricking CIA. Khara was on their radar for the past year as one the biggest global distributors of meth.

He had to listen to the rage of the DEA superior when Finn explained that he had killed a DEA agent. Lancaster's death was too easy for the traitor. Thank God for Uncle Harry's and Richard Dean's influence, Finn didn't have to leave the hotel and continued to get updates on Sophie, Tariq, and Lars.

Crossing the enormous sitting room, Finn headed to the master bedroom. His body went alert and stiff by the idea of waking a warm, sleepy Sophie.

He carefully opened the door to the master bedroom but from the hallway light, he could see that the still-made king-size bed was empty. He crossed the hallway to the next gigantic bedroom which was also empty. For a nanosecond, Finn's brain went to a bad place, but he knew Sophie had been guarded the entire time he was gone.

Reeves and his team would have notified him if Sophie had left the penthouse. He headed to the third bedroom, the uptick in his breathing echoing in the dark silence.

He pushed the door open to find the bedside lamp still on with Sophie, in her reindeer pajamas, asleep upright with a sleeping Tariq tucked under her arm, and an iPad on her lap, and the horror of the last hours vanished.

During the interrogation by the CIA, who initially treated him as if he were a suspect, Finn questioned why he did the thankless job. But seeing Sophie and Tariq safe from men like Khara and Lancaster gave him the reason. He was one lucky bastard to get to come home to Sophie.

Using his SEAL stealth, Finn closed the iPad that was open to *Harry Potter*, turned off the light, and then carefully extricated Tariq from Sophie before lifting Sophie into his arms, to pull the covers over Tariq.

Sophie moaned when he held her tight against his chest. She smelled of citrus, Sophie, and warm woman who needed the refuge of calm sleep after a terrible day with the prospect of her important talk in a few hours. He needed to keep his libido in check.

The pleasure of having her body close would have to be enough. He couldn't resist fondling her tantalizing ass as he walked her to their room. Hell, he was a man walking a narrow tightrope of love and primal lust. He pulled back the tightly tucked spread and sheets on the king-size bed, surprised that Sophie continued her light snoring.

He slowly positioned her under the sheet and pulled the cover to her chin, kissing her lightly when he really wanted to suck on her lower lip and wake her to suck on all his favorite parts. She mumbled and rolled to her side, her light snuffle undisturbed. Time to hit a cold shower since he was rock hard with no relief in sight.

Fifteen minutes later, he was clean and a bit more relaxed as he crawled into bed next to Sophie. Hoping he could sleep, he pulled her against him, resisting the urge to strip her out of those damn pajamas. Sophie moaned, snuggled closer, and threw her leg over his.

Suddenly he wasn't tired or relaxed by her leg's proximity. He forced himself to close his eyes, knowing that she was exhausted and didn't need any mauling tonight.

He drifted off until he was awoken by a most vivid dream of Sophie's mouth on him. The incredible sensation was so real in his half-conscious brain he hoped to never wake. He was close to having a wet-dream like some volatile teenager, when he heard the light laugh.

"Payback, Jenkins."

He opened his eyes to a fantasy fulfilled. Naked Sophie with curls rubbing along his chest, her lips stretched wide over him, her hands wrapped around his rigid length, smiling, her eyes sparkling in arousal. He didn't dare to blink, afraid it was an illusion. He was breathless and speechless.

"My God, Soph."

His hips arched when she ran her tongue beneath the sensitive flesh of his engorged head.

She giggled, enjoying having him at her mercy with every lick and suck. His balls drew up tight, and he could feel the orgasm tingling up his spine. But tonight was to be about Sophie. Before she could react, he flipped her on her back. It was almost comical as shock registered on her face.

"I need to taste you, honey. All I've been thinking about was how sweet you taste, and I'm the lucky guy who gets you whenever I want." Torturously, slowly, he traced a path down her soft, glowing body, avoiding the distraction of the pink, hard nipples he wanted to take into his mouth... Later.

Instead, he scattered kisses along each thigh before going for the epicenter. He buried his face between her thighs, his tongue delving through the damp folds before finding the taut bud. He flicked his tongue over her, loving her moans. "Oh, my God, Finn."

He was relentless, suckling her and then flicking rapidly, then delving his tongue into her heat. She arched her back and dug her fingers into his head. "Please, Finn."

"Payback, honey."

"Finn, not now." Her breath came in ragged pants as she begged, "Please... Please..."

And he felt the quiver of her flesh against his tongue. One last flick and she went over, pulling on his hair and screaming his name as she rode the wave.

He had to be inside her. He wanted to feel her pulsating around him, squeezing him. He rose between her thighs and plunged deep. "Forgive me, Soph. We'll go slow later."

Feeling her hot and wet molded around him took him right to the brink. He could blow right now.

She lifted her legs around his waist, her heels digging into his back and pulled his head down to thrust her tongue in and out of his mouth. She ate at his mouth in desperation.

Sophie, ravenous and demanding, her muscles rippling around him, was sublime. He pulled out almost all the way and then plunged back, deep and hard, and lifting her hips between his hands. And then he did it again and again until her nails were digging into his back and begging.

He didn't stop, his tongue thrusting with hers, in rhythm with their primal dance. Their bodies, slick with sweat, their shared labored breaths, her tremors squeezing him. He refused to give into his ferocious need. He wanted to share the moment with her. He unwrapped her legs from around his waist and pushed them higher, her legs over his shoulders, making his penetration deeper. And then he pumped into her, filling her with his seed as she raked his back with her sharp nails.

He collapsed on top of her, not able to move after his fierce and savage release.

He raised his head to look into her eyes. After the day she had, he acted like some dumb-ass, conquering Viking.

"Was I too rough?" He pulled out of her slowly, and rolled to the side, pulling her into his arms, tugging the blanket around them.

Her eyes were soft and her lips red from his demanding kisses, her curls spread across the pillow. "I was just about to ask you the same thing. You didn't hurt yourself, did you? You're going to have scratches on your back."

A deep laugh built in his chest, resonating in the empty space that didn't see a lot of laughter. "Sophie Dean, I can't live without you."

"Ditto, Finn. You're the man for me. Always was and always will be."

He was lost by her sincere declaration. He could only offer her his sworn promise—to love her faithfully as long as he lived.

He took her hand and looked into her eyes to declare himself. "Sophie, I love you. I can't imagine ever being apart from you. I've decided to give up the teams."

Sophie bolted upright. "What? You can't quit. You have eighteen months left. Your team needs you. You're the leader. They're like your brothers."

"I have brothers in Seattle. And I'm going to take over for Uncle Harry. I'll have total control over your protection 24/7 so no machete wielding Pakistani criminal can get close to you again."

"That's unfair. What are the chances of that every happening again?"

"With you in the equation…" Her forehead furrowed, her lips pinched. She was easy to get a rise out of.

"Very funny." She reached to pinch his chest, but he was quicker. He grabbed her hand and placed her soft hand over his heart. "No pinching, you little spitfire. Use your words."

"Finn Jenkins. I'm using my words right now. I love you. And you're not quitting the teams because of me." She draped her slender leg over his thigh and snuggled her head under his arm. "Will work it out. That's what people do who love each other."

EPILOGUE

Finn stood at the back of the auditorium while Sophie gave closing remarks to conclude the three-day summit. She wore a fitted, blue business suit that matched her violet blue eyes. Her bouncy curls were held tightly in the back of her neck in some sort of low ponytail. He preferred them loose and spread across his chest. He had never seen her in business attire, but she looked prim and proper and sexy as hell. All he could think about was getting her out of the suit, but the presence of her father standing nearby interrupted the fantasy just as Finn started peeling Sophie out of the tight skirt.

To not draw attention away from Sophie, Dean arrived after Sophie began her speech and stood in the back next to Finn.

Sophie's round face glowed with compassion as she encouraged the wealthy attendees to donate. The applause was thunderous as the audience stood as she finished her speech.

"I'm glad she's decided to take over the leadership of the foundation. Her mother would be very proud." Finn and Dean watched Sophie hug Yasra and then Tariq who were seated in the front row, before the crowd gathered around her. Finn wasn't in full-vigilant, protective mode with Aiden and Jordan next to Sophie and Sten at the front of the hall.

"You're taking the boy and his aunt to Orcas Island later today? But what is your take on this Marine who they are going to stay with?"

"Nothing suspicious in his background check. He has a large spread of land by Doe Bay with separate cabins for when he runs the retreats for wounded soldiers. And since he runs mostly summer programs, Yasra and Tariq can stay until their visa status gets sorted out. Thank you for calling the State department on their behalf. I know Sophie really appreciates your effort." True to form in the way he approached his business, Dean was dogmatic in trying to heal the rift between him and his daughters.

Dean shrugged as if everyone had his connections. "Isn't it the damnedest thing that the boy is from one of the richest families in Pakistan? And just like Sophie to befriend a child whose uncle was trying to murder the child. She seems to attract danger wherever she goes."

"I don't think that's fair to Sophie." Finn bristled. This was not the way he planned to have "the conversation" with Dean. But no one was allowed to slam Sophie, even her powerful father. "She's..."

"No need to defend Sophie to me. I know what a gem she is. The same kind, gentle spirit as her mother." Dean stared into the distance, lost in thought. An unusual attitude.

Finn fully understood Dean's vulnerability. Finn didn't know if he'd ever totally recover from the moment of Khara's machete against Sophie's throat.

"But I'd like to take a little credit for her feistiness. She really stomped the murderer's foot so you could take a shot? It's going to take a while for me to recover from that visual."

"Trust me. It's something I'm not going to forget."

The men laughed together for the first time since Finn had met the Dean family.

"Sir, there hasn't been time to speak with you. And if I may speak frankly, it is great that you and Sophie are finding a way to be daughter and father. But you must know, I plan to ask Sophie to marry me despite your disapproval. I know you don't consider me the type of husband you wanted for your daughter. I'll never ask Sophie to choose between us. She loves you too much. But I love her, and I will always take care of her."

Uncharacteristically Dean belly-laughed and whacked Finn on the back. "Sophie already told me that she is moving to San Diego with you until your Navy contract is up. She doesn't want you to leave the SEALs until you're ready. It was part of the negotiation of her taking over the foundation. She's quite a skilled negotiator."

"But I haven't…we haven't decided…"

Dean chuckled. "Sophie said it took you so long to tell her how you felt that if she waited for you…"

Finn spotted Sophie making her way toward them. Her eyes were sparkling like the sassy, little girl of childhood when she had outsmarted the Jenkins boys. And Finn never minded losing to Sophie as a boy or now. Her shining eyes gleamed as she tugged on her lower lip in excitement.

"Daddy, what are you two laughing about?"

"I'm entertained by how long it took for you two to figure out you were perfect for each other. There were times Harry and I weren't sure if you'd ever realize."

Sophie wrapped her arm around Finn's waist, and tilted her head to the side. "Some of us are slower…" She giggled, her grin spreading across her face.

Finn was tempted to throw her over his shoulder and take her upstairs. But not exactly the best move with his future father-in-law near. "Payback, Soph."

"You promise?" Sophie's sexy purr had Finn close to not caring about Dean's proximity.

Dean coughed into his hand. "If you two will excuse me, I see Bill."

"Are you ready to go to Orcas Island?" Finn couldn't control the gruffness or the way his body wound up real tight.

Sophie giggled. "Third time's the charm, Finn Jenkins."

Enjoy an excerpt from

MISSION:
impossible to
RESIST

THE
IMPOSSIBLE
MISSION
SERIES

BESTSELLING AUTHOR
JACKI DELECKI

CHAPTER ONE

Jordan Dean couldn't catch a break. There was no escaping the unwanted and, more than likely uninvited, guests this evening. Now Morley Townsend was in the receiving line. Her sister would never have invited Jordan's ex, because Sophie knew exactly how Jordan felt about the possessive, self-absorbed millionaire. Morley was probably here as part of another of their father's elaborate realignments of the people he saw as chess pieces.

How could an evening dedicated to global peace end up seething with such hostility, resentment, and homicidal urges? And she'd only been here about twenty minutes.

Jordan pivoted—intent on escaping to the balcony before Morley spotted her—and walked straight into a very big, very solid, very muscular wall. The sudden impact set her wobbling. The way this evening was going, she should have stayed in her flats.

The solid, muscular wall grabbed her elbows with hot, rough hands and held on until she was steadier.

"Running from a fight?" His voice was polished, smooth, and smoky, like the fifty-year-old Scottish single malt whisky Morley liked to go on about ad nauseam.

Jordan looked up...and up...into penetrating aquamarine eyes. A darker blue circle rimmed each iris, like a ring around an outer planet.

"Fight?" Her voice came out high-pitched and strangled.

He leaned closer and confided as an aside, as if they were well-acquainted, "First the itsy woman you nailed with your shoe. I was hoping to see more. And now, from the way you're high-tailing it away from the door, I'd say you're avoiding Mr. Zippity Slick..." He tipped his head toward her ex.

She twisted around to see Morley run his hand over his perfect hair, held in place by his designer clay pomade.

"Zippity Slick?" She could barely contain an unladylike snort, and the simultaneous urge to burst into hysterical giggles. Not the image Morley was aiming for with his pricey hair product.

Her muscular wall grinned, softening the razor-sharp angles of his cheekbones and making his light eyes even lighter. "An angry ex?"

Jordan's mind raced, trying to keep up with their off-kilter exchange. This was the strangest conversation she could ever remember having, made more distracting because here was a man who easily put Chris Hemsworth to shame, with his shredded body and *blue-flame-of-intensity* eyes surrounded by inky black lashes.

What he was he playing at?

"Nailed it, didn't I?" His warm, minty breath brushed against her cheek when he chuckled.

Jordan stared up into the enormous man's piercing eyes, practically baking in his heat and virility. "Let go of me, or I'll call over my bodyguard." She hated that her voice came out puny and tinny.

He waited a second too long to release her arms, then moved in close, too close, further invading her private space. "You've got to be kidding." He crossed his arms and grinned, his eyes alight with amusement and a challenge. "Go ahead. Call him."

She quickly scanned the hall, looking for Harry and the crew who guarded her and her sister 24/7.

"Your bodyguard is sick. And you haven't noticed that he isn't here, have you?"

Her heart kicked into tachycardia speeding out of control. "Harry is sick?"

"Not Harry...Pete, the man who regularly guards you. You didn't notice, did you?"

Jordan searched for Pete, a middle-aged, retired policeman who was a regular member of her security detail. He hadn't been at his post, which this evening was at the door downstairs, vetting everyone who entered the building.

Relief surged through her when she spotted Harry, who was standing by the door wearing his rumpled navy blue suit and the burgundy Armani tie she gave him for his birthday.

Mr. Mountain shook his head. "Unbelievable. You have absolutely no situational awareness."

"Shows how much you know." Situational awareness. She had it in spades—no, in sharp-edged diamonds. She was hyper-aware of Sophie's discomfort when greeting Rob Boyer, an associate of their father's and married man who had been hitting on Sophie since she was sixteen...and of Laura Stuliley cornering Sarah Sorenson's husband...and the tension between the elderly Dr. Levin and his hottie young bride.

Jordan wanted to defend herself, but she had a feeling he wouldn't be impressed.

And she had noticed Pete was absent from the downstairs entrance earlier, before her little tête–à–tête with Georgette. But, honestly, how much risk could there be while socializing in a private room, in a private club, guarded by her family's private security firm? Especially since Harry was here.

And who the hell was this man to criticize her...situational awareness...anyway?

"Who are you? I know you weren't invited tonight."

"Stand out, do I?" The edge was back in his voice, his granite jaw getting tighter with every word.

Interesting. Mr. Chiseled was sensitive?

Jacki Delecki is a bestselling romantic suspense author whose stories are filled with heart-pounding adventure, danger, intrigue, and romance.

Contemporary romantic suspense **Impossible Mission**, features Special Force Operatives; **Grayce Walters**, contemporary romantic suspense follows a Seattle animal acupuncturist with a nose for crime; and **The Code Breakers**, portrays Regency suspense set against the backdrop of the Napoleonic Wars. Delecki's stories reflect her lifelong love affair with the arts and history. When not writing, she volunteers for Seattle's Ballet and Opera Companies, and leads children's tours of Pike Street Market.

To learn more about Jacki and her books and to be the first to hear about giveaways, join her newsletter found on her website. Follow her on Facebook Jacki Delecki; Twitter @jackidelecki; Bookbub jacki-delecki; Goodreads Jacki_Delecki.

http://www.JackiDelecki.com.

Made in the USA
Columbia, SC
14 July 2022

63465990R00121